Ten-Cent Man

GITE TAMAR

BTW LLC

To those afraid of speaking up, cleanse the frivolous stuff
that riddles your tongue and claim victory over the uphill
mental battle you have won.

Acknowledgment

Thank you to my dear Grandfather, Lawerence Wright; you will always be with me in my waking life. I'm sure you are in the great heavens above, riding on horseback with the icons you love. Rest in peace, Boppa.

Contents

One

Not Just A Cowboy

1869, Whittletown

A stray tumbleweed manically rolls through the dusty terrain; its jostling movement similar to the erratic motion of an unhitched train. Each performance of the traveling debris creates a faint trail of sweeping dust that adds character to the landscape's desolation. As the clustered twigs embark on the long journey across the desert floor, an oddity of built civilization lures the parched bones to take a closer look.

Inspired by hopes of life, the single skitter quickens its speed to investigate the distant structure. As it reaches the architecture, it finds an opening and squeezes between a gap in the boards of an oak picket fence. Inside the isolation of the barricade stands a curious structure--a small white chapel with clusters of gingerbread shingles draped along the roofline and windows constructed from multi-colored pieces of stained glass. A single eave houses a new bevy of cobweb spirals, and the sinister ambiance created by the arachnids' recent occupancy, reveals the structure's harsh reality of abandonment.

Gusty air currents carry the ball of misguided dust further across the terrain. Spurts of wind whistle as they grace the sides of the building's freshly painted baton-board siding. Dancing around the chapel, its jarring traveling motions reveal a mysterious graveyard stationed behind the dead silent edifice. The ancient burial ground of chipping tombstones contrasts the church's exterior, with each chunk of carved stone partaking in the lineup appearing more weathered than the last.

Contrary to the parched presentation of the ancient stone markers, hills of moist soil rest atop the dusty ground, signifying the addition of new graves. The last burial in the lineup is marked by a piece of wormholed wood carved in the shape of a crooked cross. In front of the nameless marker, a newly excavated pit awaits a body, and next to the trench sits a monumental heap of dampened silt. A worn shovel stabs the top of the soil like a flag to claim hold over the territory.

Sounds of low moans echoing from human lips reverberate in unison with the slight gusts of wind. As the tumbleweed continues its journey, it skips across the freshly packed barrows protecting the peacefully sleeping bodies of the deceased. The abrasive tune of a snoring man breaks over the lonely acreage, adding a base-toned accent to the wind's whistling orchestration.

With no hope of changing course, the ticklegrass falls unannounced into the last grave's opening and lands on the man taking a nap. His dirty hand appears rugged and reveals a plethora of blisters as it lifts from an empty bottle of whiskey. Fumbling for the pistol around his hip, he frantically swats the tumbleweed off his body and shoots a stray bullet into the clear blue sky.

As he orients himself to his surroundings, his fingers slowly tilt the brim of a dark brown cowboy hat from his eyes. Around the felt Stetson's border is a braided piece of black leather with flecks of silver that shine in the sun. His eyes are a piercing shade of ice blue and his hair is a hue of dirty blonde.

Lifting the hat from his head, he runs his fingers through each strand of greasy, messy hair. A sun-kissed lock escapes his combing digits and falls forward, gracing the tips of his eyelashes. Effortlessly slicking it into an unruly style, he lightly places the cap back on his head to shade his weary eyes.

Sitting upright, he pushes himself to the grave wall, brushes the soot from his camel-brown chaps with fringe, and flicks gritty particles from his open shirt and matching leather vest. "Goddamn. It's brighter than a pinto's coat."

Quickly tilting his hat down, he allows his hands to feel for the bottle of booze. He pulls the cork and tips the container to quench his parched lips. Not sensing a single trickle of alcohol upsets him, and he tosses the empty glass container into the sky. "Get gone."

Raising his pistol, he fires a single bullet into the airborne bottle, shattering it into a hundred pieces. The fractured glass sprinkles across his body like an unwanted rain shower, and he holds his hands up in a defensive position to shield himself. "Blam-jam bottle!" he shouts as his hands wildly swing at the attacking shards.

Annoyed by the tumbleweed watching him, his face exudes a mean glare as he lifts his dirt-packed fingernail to point at the stationary observer. "If you don't watch out, you may be next." Inching forward to intimidate the uncaring scrub brush, he braces his swaying body against the compacted dirt walls and kicks the ball of twigs with the silver spur of his dusty black cowboy boot.

A discolored piece of paper pokes out from a pile of collected debris at the base of the hole, piquing his curiosity. He leans forward to pull it from the rubbish and quickly realizes it is a wanted poster with a picture bearing an extreme likeness to him. Holding it close to his face, he admires the man's square jawline and reads the text underneath.

"Alonzo Bill... I'll be damned. That's me." As he lifts the sketched portrait to his pupils, he chuckles at the pitiful bounty offered for his capture. "Fifty cents and an extra helpin' of communion, dead or alive. I would have thought my hide'd be worth more than a couple of coins and a stale piece of bread." Folding up the yellowing paper, he tucks it away in his pocket as a souvenir.

Alonzo caresses the stubble on his tanned face and smiles. *You may be wondering how a drifter like me ended up being a wanted man. I take the commotion as flattery. My Momma always told me that if you don't ruffle the feathers of at least a dozen people in your path, you're not doing something right. Based on those truthful words, I must be doing a whole lot right in the world.*

Swiftly, he stands up to his feet and places a hand on each side of the freshly dug burial pit. Using all his strength, he heaves himself out of the earthen hole to sit next to the adjacent wooden cross.

As he admires the even row of newly dug graves, a black raven squawking interrupts his thoughts as it perches on the worn wood next to him. He turns his body to address his new acquaintance. "Hey there, friend."

The raven adjusts its spindly feet to look him directly in the eyes and answers him with a shrill squawk. Alonzo smiles. "I tell you what, loners like you and me are the best company to keep. If you don't mind excusing me for a moment, I have some unfinished business to tend to."

Alonzo stares at a shovel perched atop an enormous mound of excavated silt nearby. He helps himself to his feet while the beautiful raven remains stationary, cawing as it watches his every move. "Let's keep this between you and me. It'll be our little secret," he says as he scales the giant heap of dirt.

Working his way to the top, he tightly grips hold of the shovel's handle and draws it from the loamy hill like King Arthur's sword Excalibur. As he lifts the dull blade to the sky, he releases a tribal call from his lips and points the rusted end towards the old church house. "I'm coming for you, Reverend!" he yells.

His eyes pan to the bottom of the slope as he takes in a vast inhalation of air. Clearing his throat, he lowers himself to sit at the top edge of the mound and uses the shovel like a boat paddle to row his way down. Once at the bottom, he jumps to his feet, proudly puffs his chest toward the sky, and adjusts the brim of his hat. Both heels of his boots plant into the ground as he fixates on the white painted sides of the church. *After all the shit I've had to endure, people shouldn't want to lynch me. They should want to honor the ground my boots have touched.*

Tilting his head from left to right causes his vertebra to let out a *crack* as he stretches his neck. He takes a deep breath to center his thoughts, and before taking a step, he uses the shovel to knock the grime from each spur.

Staggering towards the eerily quiet building, he tips the brim of his hat to every grave he passes. A special acknowledgment is given to the newest additions, as he tries to perform the sign of the cross. The added effort throws him off balance, causing him to jar backward with each "Amen."

"Bill, Sue, Lou, and whoever else you may be, I condemn y'all to rest in peace. Hell, I don't know about you, but I am damn sure that is the best each of you sinners is gonna get."

Chuckling at his joke brings a warm smile across his ash-stained lips as he continues closer to the chapel. Swathed in his blissful moment, he performs a two-stepping motion with the shovel the rest of the way to the deteriorated structure.

He stops at the base of the stairs, takes a slight bow, and, being a gentleman, allows his dance partner to go up first. Following an arm's length behind, he hops each step to the top, and upon reaching the entrance, begins moving the shovel side to side as if it were conversing. "Thank you, kind sir. If only I could find a man with such honor," he says in a high-pitched tone.

Alonzo glances over his right shoulder before placing his opposite hand over his heart to address his partner. "Aw, shucks, little miss, anything for a beauty like yourself," he says with a bashful smirk.

His body stiffens, and his lean muscles flex from top to bottom over his tall stature as he wiggles his finger at the shovel. "Now, I know you think I am easy on the eyes, but there will be no funny business in there." Facing the door, he takes a glance back at the shovel. "You hear me?"

His hand moves the shovel to mimic a nodding motion. "Good."

He places his free hand on the door and turns the handle. A loud creak shatters the stagnant air as the door hinges slowly open, revealing the interior of the hallowed walls and the remnants of a massacre.

Gruesome textures and bullet holes taint every inch of the archaic structure. Scarlet handprints smear the walls, and spatter covers the pews as if a bloody rainstorm exclusively occurred within the church's confines. Sticky gore coats the aisles' floorboards like a crimson river running in the direction of the altar.

Looking down the aisle, he finds exactly what he is searching for and smiles at a decapitated man sprawled across a pew. The barely recognizable carcass wears what was once an all-white robe, and his severed head is located nearly a foot away from its born resting place. Its long beard soaks in unrelated body matter as it lies face-down in a pool of blood.

Taking a moment to secure the shovel under his arm, Alonzo walks over to the corpse, turns his eyes to the ceiling, and completes the sign of the cross. "Sorry it had to end this way, Reverend. We are all probably going to Hell after this rodeo." His left hand snatches a handful of hair from the back of the decapitated head, and, holding it an arm's length away from his face, he intently stares into its bloodshot eyes. "You're sure an ugly son of a gun, aren't ya?" he says with a chuckle.

Using his right hand, he grabs hold of the Reverend's ankle and begins dragging him to the door. As the body sweeps the floor, a trail of dark burgundy is left behind.

Alonzo takes a moment of pause, raising the man's head to his eye line. Using a patch of unsullied hair, he wipes a bead of sweat away from his brow and allows an ample grunt to release from between his pursed lips. The extra effort helps him gather momentum, and with the body in tow, he finishes his departure through the church doors.

With his hands full of the Reverend's remains, he pulls the body down the stairsteps. Loud, deep thumps ensue from the impact of the wood with the limp dead weight.

He aggressively yanks the corpse by its ankle, leaving behind a rutted path, like the trail of a serpent through a pit of mud. Steadily, he drags the butchery past the row of occupied graves. Upon reaching the edge of the last and only open hole, he lets loose his grip.

Wanting to rid himself of the head, he swings it back and forth, then tosses it into the pit. It impacts the bottom of the dirt-packed cavern with a hollow thud. He nudges the decapitated remains and gory bits over the grave's edge using his foot, and they willingly comply in joining the severed head.

Alonzo removes the shovel from under his armpit and begins unloading the pile of dirt back into the hole.

Right now, you may be wondering what the heck is going on. Well, it's simple. My name is Alonzo Bill, and you just saw me on the clock. Y'all, I am a cowboy--more like a cowboy vigilante of the unknown.

If I were in your boots, I would be wondering how someone with my good looks got roped into such a bizarre profession. Let me tell you, it is far from an easy ride. You may not believe in the paranormal and unknown--trust me, I was once there myself.

Why don't I take you back in time, to the day when my way of looking at things changed? It served as one of those coming to Jesus moments.

I first got lassoed into this line of work thinking it was an easy way to swindle greenbacks, but boy, was I wrong. This rodeo is real, and the body you are watching me bury... well, we will come back to this here body in two shakes of a lamb's tail.

But first, I'm going to make you a believer.

Two

Itching For A Drink

1864, Wild West Saloon

Alonzo Bill pushes open the swinging shutter doors of the Branding Iron Saloon and enters dressed in all-black leather chaps, coat, and cowboy boots. Perched on top of his head is a black ten-gallon Stetson hat made of beaver felt and adorned with a silver braided-horsehair hatband. The first three buttons lay open on his long-sleeved button-down black shirt, and its flawless tailoring affirms his broad shoulders and slender waistline. The lowest part of the opening exposes the tip of a scar that continues down the midline of his chest. Every inch of Alonzo's lean, muscular body is pristinely clad. Not a single hair ventures to step out of place unless purposely positioned to accent his rugged good looks.

Alonzo stands in the entry as if waiting for a round of applause as he scans his surroundings. Although the environment is dusty, it does not take the liberty to taint his cocky demeanor.

The sight of a bartender neurotically polishing glassware behind an ornately carved wooden bar creates a sense of peace in his gut. Shelves of colorfully tinted glass bottles of alcohol line the bar's back wall like a muted rainbow. Each bottle immaculately accents the ledges, which are polished with beeswax, and the sight makes his clenched jaw release a calming sigh.

Positioned around the room are a copious number of candles laid out in the shape of a pentagram. Every fiery wick protruding from the wax flickers notes of murky gray and melts red candle wax to the dusty floor's battered wooden planks.

As the itching sensation of his thirst builds, his attention stays enticed by the barkeep's hypnotic cleaning motions. Distracted by alcohol-induced tunnel vision, he pays no mind to the weird room lighting. The pace of his rambunctious march across the rustic floor causes the heels of his spurs to tap against the ground, causing jingling sounds to ring through the saloon's dark corners.

His lips smirk as his attention strays to the window's peculiar choice of make-shift curtains and unusual room organization. Cream-colored bed sheets cover each window, impaled by rusty nails sticking out of each corner's edge. Instead of chairs and tables set up for patrons, the middle of the room is bare. Underneath the crude drapes sit muddled stacks of round wooden tables and chipped chairs barricading the openings.

Alonzo Bill finds the dramatic presentation unnecessary and comical. His mind ponders the scene. *Are they trying to keep bears out? This is the most bamboozling saloon I've ever set eyes on.* He chuckles at the thought.

Finishing his whiskey-enticed march, he takes a seat at the far end of the bar made from a large piece of carved fir.

The barkeep's creased skin and grayed temples reveal him to be around sixty years of age. His nose sits above a perfectly twisted salt-and-pepper handlebar mustache that slightly overhangs the top part of his upper lip. A red-and-white striped shirt and coffee-colored trousers peep from underneath his light-brown service apron. The bartender intentionally disregards the squeaking sound from the swiveling stool as the lone cowboy takes a seat. Ignoring the new patron, he feigns distraction by repetitively drying the same glistening glass.

Alonzo has no reservation in displaying his annoyance at the blatant lack of service, and loudly clears his throat to capture the man's attention. The abrupt coughing catches the older man off-guard, causing him to startle. He reluctantly tilts the pupils of his eyes to peer past the top frame of his wireframed reading glasses. Noticing his captive audience, Alonzo harshly taps the pointer finger of his right hand against the top of the table.

The barkeep recognizes the motion and places the polished glass back onto the shelf next to the rest. He peruses the contents of the top shelf and pulls down a bottle of moonshine. Grabbing a shot glass, he pours an overflowing jigger and slides the drink to the end of the counter. Alonzo's eyes grow with excitement as the contents slosh over the glass's edge.

Wasting no time, he leans forward to fetch the drink. Once it's in his grasp, he chugs the fiery liquid like a fiend and slams the empty glass down on the table. His face forms a theatrical cringe from the burn of the liquid sliding down his throat, and his shoulders dramatically shudder. The bartender is not entertained by the outlandish attempt for attention.

Alonzo lifts the brim of his hat from his eyes, revealing a five o'clock shadow from his cheeks to his chin. Once again, he swiftly taps his finger against the table with a stoic smile. "C'mon, now, Bar Dog, no need to look sour," he says as he slides the empty glass back in his direction. "Give me another snort of that liquid courage."

The bartender watches the glass slowly come to a stop in front of him and begrudgingly turns around to retrieve the bottle of moonshine from the shelf. When his back turns, Alonzo rolls his eyes. Leisurely making his way with bottle in hand to the waiting glass, the bartender pops the cork and pours another shot. Instead of placing the bottle back on the shelf, he leaves it on the bar. "You'd better slow down, now... I reckon you'll be as full as a tick after this," he says, annoyed, as his hand slides the full glass towards Alonzo.

Two sure ways to ruffle Alonzo's feathers are to control his independent way of thinking and to eliminate his capacity to drink freely. He raises his hand to silence the barkeep out of irritation that someone is giving him the what-for. His eyes regard the glass descending in his direction. He snatches the drink, and a small amount spills over the countertop as he lifts it in the air to mock the bartender. Plastering on a condescending smile, he snaps back in response, "I reckon your name starts with a C."

Tapping his head with his opposite hand, he tries to wiggle the remembrance of his name out of his brain. The barkeeper attempts to interrupt to prompt his memory. Alonzo makes a grunt with his throat to stop him. "Hold your fire, Bar Dog. I'm mustering it up," he spouts, cutting him off.

The bartender is irritated by the guessing game and quietly moves back to re-polishing glasses on the counter. Even though he delivers no more interjection, Alonzo attempts to get a rise by raising his hand higher, as if to silence him. "Rein it in and hobble your lip. I'm gonna need more of this firewater in me," he says.

Placing the glass to his lips, he chugs the entire sum of liquid and cringes. "Sure burns like Hell. You know, the best ideas always come to me after a drink. Yessiree, a little liquor is the best way to clear my mind."

He scratches his fingers against his felt cowboy hat and enthusiastically lifts the empty glass to signal an idea. The Bartender ignores him and continues polishing. Alonzo aggressively points at him with a loud snap of his fingers. "Cooper! Wow, wee, that's it. Your name is Cooper," he loudly announces.

Impressed by his guess, the bartender pauses and sets a shiny glass back on the counter with the rest. Still a bit puzzled over the correct deduction, he raises his eyebrows and nods his head.

Alonzo laughs at his look of surprise. "You almost had me as mad as a March Hare," he says while sliding his empty glass back down the bar towards Cooper for a refill. Fueled by excitement, he shoves the small cup with too much force, causing it to overshoot the counter and shatter on the floor around Cooper's feet.

The harsh sound disrupts the air, and he scrutinizes the mess surrounding him with utter disbelief. Cooper closes his eyes tightly, winces, and takes a deep breath to calm his annoyance. Watching the bartender's face comically turn a light shade of red makes Alonzo Bill feel accomplished.

The sound of his unsuccessful attempt at holding back his building snickers makes Cooper's blood boil. Opening his eyes to face the disrespect, he glares with daggers to show his irritation. "You sure are an odd stick, aren't you?" he says. Tightly clenching his jaw, he crawls on his knees, picking up the shards of glass.

Alonzo, feeling not an ounce of shame for his actions, leans over the wooden slab to gain a clearer view. With a mischievous smirk plastered across his face, he whistles a catcall and obnoxiously heckles him. Cooper hears his growing belligerent slurs from the alcohol and, knowing there is no reasoning with intoxication, refrains from looking up.

Alonzo quickly grows bored and changes the subject. "When's that hussy getting here, anyway?" he inquires. Without waiting for an answer, he aggressively taps the top of the table with his finger to request another drink.

Cooper completes cleaning up the remaining shards of glass and throws them into the trash. Trying to ignore his ignorance, he pauses to formulate a response. Upon regaining his composure, he sternly fixes his stare on Alonzo. "I'll give you some advice: Don't let the Preacher catch you talking about her like that."

The change of seriousness in the inflection of his voice causes Alonzo to slap his leg as he laughs harder. His laughter is so raucous that he turns in his chair and, for the first time, catches the unusual display of burning candles lighting the room. Still oblivious to the effects of his actions, he assumes Cooper has only reacted with annoyance due to the theatrical melting-wax spectacle surrounding him, and he leans forward to let him in on a secret. "Oh, I know, I know. Sure, as Hell, not trying to copper my bet," he says as his finger motions to a single candle.

Continuing to make a spectacle, his eye releases a trail of winks, his shoulders shrug to his ears, and his face gives an appearance of eating an unripe lime. "If you catch my drift," he says.

Cooper stands stationary across the counter and squints at Alonzo, making it clear that his carefree nature concerning the situation does not amuse him. Snatching the bottle of moonshine from the bar, he corks it and places it back on the shelf. "They should be down directly," Cooper says as he takes another long glance at Alonzo's swaying body. "You sure you're not too roistered?" he asks.

Alonzo Bill thinks he's joking and slaps his palm against the bar. "Come on now, Cooper, I don't want no fuss. I'm not even a little jingled; I'm just jawing with you."

Leaning closer, he tries to connect on a deeper level with the Barkeep to sway his judgment. Extending his finger, he motions him to come closer with a warm smile. "We've known each other for a while now, Coop."

Hearing the words fall from his mouth confuses Cooper, and he blankly stares at him in silence. Alonzo continues to grasp for commonality and squashes the quiet moment with his uncomplicated attempt. "So, that means you'll always lay it out straight for me, right, Coop?" he asks.

Feeling oddly sorry for his ignorance, Cooper feeds into his whim. Slowly walking toward Alonzo, he leans over the counter, reluctantly places a hand on top of his shoulder, and pats it lightly in a consoling fashion. "If you pay the drink tab you owe, then sure, partner, I'll give it to you straight. I'll answer whatever question you can muster up."

After taking a moment of solace to digest the entirety of the barkeep's words, he bobs his head to show his understanding. Even though Alonzo knows the empty condition of the leather money belt secured around his waist, he puts on a show and frantically fumbles for his phantom coins.

Watching his diligent search for coins gives the barkeep a momentary glimmer of hope. He refrains from movement as the cattle roper holds up a finger to signal him to wait for his payment, and the hopeful anticipation causes him to develop a new respect for the man. While waiting patiently for Alonzo to hand him the proper amount of cash, he keeps his hand extended in front of him.

Upon his deepest dig into the pouch, Alonzo sticks out his tongue and licks his bottom lip to add a look of concentration to his bold attempt. Finally, his hand retreats with a handful of contents. Looking the barkeep dead in the eye, he slaps the payment into his open palm with pride.

The grand gesture puts a slight grin on Cooper's face as he retracts his grasping hand, but immediately upon uncurling his fingers, his eyes are met with the sight of a foreign coin and an empty rusted tobacco tin. His change of heart turns to loathing as his pupils stare with frustration at the bamboozling contents bestowed upon him.

Trying to divert the barkeeper's obvious irritation at the low-ball offer, Alonzo boastfully acts like nothing is wrong. He is confident that if he pretends everything is just water under the bridge, he might still trick the bartender into giving him the information he yearns for.

"So, the Preacher's daughter you spoke of..." Quieting his voice, he pauses and scans from left to right to check that no one is listening in on their conversation. "Is she possessed, or is it just a woman thing?"

Still scrutinizing the pile of trash in his hand, Cooper listens to the insensitive question and tries to lighten the mood with a sarcastic laugh.

Noticing the bartender's lack of response and disinterest in giving him the information, Alonzo switches his approach to be more lighthearted by covering his inquiry with a friendly joke. He places both hands on the bar to establish a mutual connection. "Just shooting the shit here, but we both know how women can sometimes be." Still receiving no response, not even a chuckle for the commentary he thought funny, he becomes antsy sitting on the squeaky bar stool and pivots it from side to side. As Cooper remains unemotionally staring at his handful of junk, Alonzo rolls his eyes and gestures with his fingers in a circular motion, signaling that the man is loco.

Observing the action out of the corner of his vision does not sit well with the barkeep. He holds the unusually structured stray coin to his eyes and places it between his two back molars to check the density. The solid-gold quality pleasantly surprises him, and he swiftly hides it away in his apron pocket.

Alonzo ignores what is happening in front of him and stops swiveling his seat. He attempts to switch his approach in dealing with the man and shifts his mannerisms to appear more subdued. Leaning closer, he calculatingly presses Cooper for more information. "The way the religious man explained her had me scared to my wits' end," he says.

Cooper doesn't buy his ploy for a single second, and his head turns at the pace of molasses to leer at him. The cowboy's eyes grow vast with excitement as he perceives the action of the passive stare as a form of validation. To keep the supposed momentum going, he flips the narrative and clambers to join the interaction as if they agree.

As he maintains eye contact with Alonzo, Cooper slaps the empty can of tobacco on the hewn-wood saloon counter in front of him. His hand slowly pushes the rusted tin back towards the cowboy, causing a scratching screech to resonate through the room. The sound causes' Cooper's eye to twitch lightly underneath his stoic countenance, and Alonzo relishes the payback. "All the tales are true," Cooper says.

He removes his hand from the top of the tin, and Alonzo stares down at the canister. Assuming the barkeep is pulling his leg, he allows a chuckle to build in his throat. Raising his pupils, he catches Cooper's stale exterior and realizes he'd misread the nuance of his statement. The cowboy snatches the empty tin and places it back in his spacious money pouch.

He opens his mouth to break the silence, but is stopped by the sound of heavy footsteps descending the nearby staircase. Each abrupt footfall and connected creak create a sinister echo that rings through the room. Cooper turns his head to view the stairs. Alonzo follows suit, and both gentlemen fall silent as their heads snap to stare toward the escalating sound.

After what seems like an eternity, the silhouette of a man of the cloth appears. Cooper lets a whisper out from the corner of his mouth. "I reckon that there is Preacher Boone. I'm sure he is more than willing to answer your questions." The advice causes Alonzo to gulp intently as he analyzes the approaching man.

As Preacher Boone finishes his last step down the broad staircase, he is illuminated by the flickering candles. Dark circles and bags plague his eyes, and his face droops with emotional wear. The man's ghost-white skin is clad in week-old Reverend attire. As his feet wearily stagger nearer to the bar, it becomes clear by his moderate wrinkles that he is nearing fifty years of age. His proximity, combined with radiance from the candlelight, reveals a putrid green stain that runs from the collar of his shirt to his belt buckle. His wide-set brown eyes are abnormally plastered open, giving every impression he has seen a ghost.

Mimicking the living dead, he stands at the far end of the bar and blankly gazes at one of the sheet-covered windows across the room. He slowly places his shaky palms against the counter for stability and lightly taps two fingers.

Amused by the man's dramatic presentation, Alonzo inappropriately stares and shakes his head with a lighthearted chuckle. The Preacher startles at the sound of his laughter and slowly turns to gape in his direction, revealing the full extent of the vicious blackened circles staining the skin surrounding his vacant look. The cowboy seizes his opportunity to break the ice. "What in God's sweet gravy happened to you?"

Looking back at Cooper, the Preacher ignores the insensitive nature behind the question. The cold reaction causes Alonzo to scan the bar for a distraction from the awkward silence, while the pit of his stomach gurgles for another drink to take the edge off the situation. Without a moment of pause, the bartender races to the second shelf and grabs a bottle of premium aged whiskey. As he reaches for a shot glass, he glances at the Preacher's disheveled appearance and changes his choice to a tumbler.

Alonzo's eyes bulge with disbelief at the better treatment offered to the Preacher. Sloshing alcohol settling in the glass causes his fingers to twitch against his thigh. Lured by the smell of the wafting liquid, his eyes fixate on the generous pour. As Cooper brings the brimming glass to the middle of the bar, the cowboy stands to his feet. Flicking his wrist, Cooper slides the drink towards the Preacher, and Alonzo frantically rushes to intercept it. Mid-scramble, he realizes he won't make it in time to snatch the whiskey for himself, and returns to his seat to sulk.

The Preacher grabs the glass and swiftly gulps every drop. Hearing the empty glass hitting the timber countertop provokes Alonzo, and he throws his hand into the air to get the barkeep's attention. "C'mon now, Coop, Coop," he says as he stands to his feet. Knowing Preacher Boone calls the shots in the establishment, he makes his way across to him.

With his hands braced against the bar, the preacher stays standing as Alonzo pulls up a seat next to him and playfully begins nudging his side to rally camaraderie. Receiving an anticlimactic reaction, Alonzo directs his attention toward the man harboring the alcohol and, pointing at himself, tries lightening the mood with a joke. "I thought they usually serve lookers like myself first," he boisterously spouts through his laughter. Continuing to cackle drunkenly, he takes a gander at the other two men for validation and is met with sheer silence. He ceases his attempt and turns to observe Preacher Boone finally take a seat.

As the Preacher's weight transfers to the wooden stool, his head slumps into his hands and his fingers firmly clutch his messy hair to pray. "Dear Lord, forgive me, for I have sinned. Dear Lord, forgive me, for I have sinned. Dear Lord, forgive me, for I have sinned. Please, dear Lord, forgive me, for I have sinned," he mumbles. He clutches his hair tighter, as if trying to punish himself.

Thinking his behavior to be odd, Alonzo Bill's head snaps towards Cooper to see if he perceives it the same way. The Barkeep avoids eye contact, picks up a rag, and frantically begins polishing the bar's wooden finishes. Taking matters into his own hands, Alonzo tries to cheer up the mood by persuading the Preacher out of his slump. "Jesus Christ, you sound like a broken fiddle. What in the Hell has gotten into you, Preacher?"

The words strike a nerve with the praying man, and he slowly stops his repetitive words to lift his head. Annoyed by the inebriate sitting next to him, he directs his attention straight to Cooper. "Are you sure he's qualified?"

The bartender stops his cleaning to glance at the cowboy before addressing the concern. Alonzo meets his eye contact and smirks with a wave. Cooper reluctantly turns his focus back to the Preacher and nods his head without releasing a single word. Picking up where he left off, he polishes the bar's wood to make himself look busy and motions his head towards Alonzo. "I reckon you mean the one that is painting his nose," he says. As he tries to cover his embarrassment for hiring the man, he speeds up his speech to soften the blow of disappointment, "Sure is, Preacher... Sure is."

Refusing to acknowledge the Preacher's uncertain reaction, he occupies himself by picking up a clean glass to polish and takes a second squint at the cowboy. "I reckon so," he says. Alonzo is oblivious to the condescending undertones and smiles at the distraught man sitting next to him.

Sensing the cowboy's stare, the Preacher releases a long sigh and slowly turns to address him. "I take it you read the entire contents of the solicitation for the job?"

Alonzo Bill scoots his stool closer, causing the wooden legs scratching against the floor to let out a shrill screech of friction. He smiles with a chuckle and loudly clears his throat. "Well, I'm here, aren't I?" he replies, flinging out his arms.

The Preacher glances at Cooper in disbelief, and they both slowly look toward the darkened staircase and shudder. Cooper shrugs, removing himself from the conversation, and returns to cleaning glasses.

Preacher Boone quickly refocuses his gaze on the stairs. Realizing he is running out of time, he recognizes no other option than to brief the clueless man sitting beside him. He places his hand against the bar and swivels his body to face him. Glaring with stern intent, he looks him directly in the eyes and lowers his voice to a loud whisper. "The little lady you are about to meet is crazier than a mangy coyote."

Unable to hold in his snicker, Alonzo's lips vibrate together, causing spit to fly into the air. "Aren't they all?" he replies. Laughing at his own joke, he playfully places his hand against the Preacher's shoulder, but swiftly retracts it when he finally recognizes his genuine concern over the situation.

Cooper spots the awkward exchange between the two and quietly moves closer to listen in on their conversation. The cowboy is relieved at the sight of the barkeep's presence. He turns his attention to him and immediately begins to tap the bar to call for a drink. "Let's cheers to that! Coop, I know your ears are burning over there, so make yourself useful and get us another round. Hell, why don't you take one with us?"

The bartender stops polishing the glass in his hand and looks toward Preacher Boone for approval. Tired of the foolishness, he apathetically waves his hand in the air for another round. "You heard the man. I feel like another round of that liquid courage counts for a fair shake," he says.

"Whatever you say, boss," Cooper says with a shrug. With a quick step, he picks up the empty jigger from in front of Alonzo and, grabbing clean glasses, pours two shots of whiskey. As he makes his way to the men, he carefully places the first drink in front of the Preacher.

Noticing the barkeep taking his time, the cowboy becomes impatient and interjects. "C'mon, barkeep, get a wiggle on," he says with a half-joking laugh.

Cooper turns toward the cowboy and spitefully scowls. Alonzo senses the animosity and lightheartedly raises his hands above his head to show a sign of surrender. He turns to his drinking partner to defuse the situation. "We go way back," he says.

Cooper slams the second shot on the table, causing part of the contents to spill over the edge of the small glass. The cowboy whispers to the Preacher to explain the hostile behavior. "Coop loves pulling my donkey's tail. "

Preacher Boone has no energy to inquire more about the matter, and lifts his glass to announce cheers. "Hope to the dear Lord above this helps make you savage as a meat axe," he slurs.

Alonzo pretends the partially empty glass and contents of the speech don't bother him. Sarcastically smiling at the barkeep, he lifts the shot into the air. "You know, I am not one you can typically shake a stick at, but like my Momma always told me, beggars can't be choosers. So, I'll drink to that!" he says. He rapidly downs the whiskey and slams the empty glass onto the table.

Waiting with anticipation, Cooper rushes to collect the empty glasses from the men before anyone can slide another onto the floor. Alonzo appears confused as the barkeep frantically begins tidying everything up.

Preacher Boone stiffens his posture as he analyzes how melted the candles surrounding them are. "We have to hurry before it awakens." The Preacher wasting no time getting to business, instantaneously jumps to his feet. Alonzo Bill turns to gawp at him while he races to the closest candle to study the flickering flame. Lowering himself to the floor, he army-crawls on all fours to look at the tiny fire.

As his face hovers an inch away from the candle's glow, the flame turns black, and his eyes grow broad with terror. Panic makes his forehead drip with sweat. "We have little time now. I reckon we only have a few ticks of my pocket watch left," he says.

Three

The Black Flame

The air is thick as pudding in the men's nostrils and exudes a smell mimicking the inner confines of a stale jail. As each second passes, the temperature grows colder, and the bartender quickens his cleaning pace. He continues scrubbing the countertop so neurotically that when the cowboy turns around, he notices the wax finish peeling away.

The sight instantly causes Alonzo's throat to be locked and loaded with a sarcastic remark, but when a quick exhalation of breath creates an unmistakable foggy cloud in the icy air, it leaves him confused to the point that he retracts his thoughts and seals his mouth shut. Trying to reach the bottom of the mystery, he waves his hand in front of his lips to break up the precipitous cloud. As the cold fog disintegrates, he can no longer hold his breath, and another one takes its place from his next exhalation.

Giving up on his mission, he looks to the sealed windows around the room and removes his cowboy hat to scratch his head to think. *There must be an open window I'm not seeing.*

His detective work is cut short by the sound of the other men's teeth chattering and kneecaps knocking together. He becomes amused by his compadres' cowardliness. Everything happening seems like a theatrical production to him, and he snickers at the other two men's panicked mannerisms. Rather than letting the oddities of the environment take hold of his psyche, he takes a spirited spin on his stool to ease the mood.

Sensing his momentum come to a stop, Alonzo changes his trajectory and playfully hops off the chair mid-twirl. He jumps to his feet, and the gravity forcefully thrusts his spurs into the hardwood floor panels. The jagged points of the rotating silver spurs create a squeal as they impact the ground.

The sound from the heels of his freshly polished cowboy boots tapping against the fir floor inspires him to jig. Without a single moment of stagnancy, he shifts his leisurely walking pace into a two-step dance, treating the eerie color of candle flames as spotlights on his cavorting limbs. At the height of his movement, he removes his pistols from the holsters slung across his hips like a vigilante and pretends to shoot the firearms into the air. Pursing his lips together, he spits out small sounds of shooting rounds through the saloon. "Pew, pew, pew."

The other men's faces are stricken white with angst as they wait for their impending doom. Engulfed by their worrisome fear, they pay no mind to the show being put on before them, which doesn't diminish his chipper tone. Enjoying his moment as the hero figure in the narrative brings him exponential joy, and he sets his sight on the Preacher, who sits mesmerized by the black flame.

He plants both of his boots and takes one final hop forward, landing next to the mysterious candle. In unison with the loud thud of his touchdown, he spins the revolvers one time on his fingers and blows a spurt of cold fog at each of the loaded barrels. Finished with his trick, he simultaneously places them back in his holsters.

He isn't frightened by the flame's presence from a bird's-eye view, so he thinks his opinion might differ if he has a closer encounter with the unique candle that haunts the other men. Brushing off the knees of his suede chaps, he lowers himself down to the level of the Preacher, closes one eye, and squints a single lid to pinpoint his focus. Bored and still not buying the spectacle, he raises his right hand to the level of his eyes and swings it through the flickering black flame as if playing with the glow. "Don't mean to be the bearer of bad news, Preacher, but I've seen this sideshow trick before," he says.

Still intently focused on the burning wick, Preacher Boone's eyes grow large with alarm. The dancing flame is the only gauge he has for when the festivities haunting each night are about to begin, and he fears that if the flame is extinguished, they will be attacked blindly without the glowing timer. Snapping his hand towards the cowboy, he tries to prompt him to retract his mocking demeanor. "Stop that! You don't know what you are doing!" Frantically swinging his arm causes his brow to create waterfalls of sweat.

Finding Alonzo's behavior irresponsible, he unintentionally joins in the festivities by taking part in a game of keep away. Alonzo snatches the red wax candle into his grasp. As the candle lifts from the floorboards, it leaves a wax ring behind in the shape of a volcano's mouth, and the sight causes the already-skittish man to lay frozen with deepening horror. Thinking of the entire affair as a witty charade, he waves the flickering candle in front of his face to fetch a better gander.

As his curious pupils try to debunk the mystery behind the mesmerizing color of the flame, his presumptuous mouth starts to spout unproven speculations. "You see now, sometimes, these candles are made with flaws that are so small even the human eye can't see them. The reason behind the darkened fire could be simple. I bet it's caused by some charcoal getting inside this here candle, and that's why it acts mighty witchy when lit," he says. His fingers twist the candle's body as he attempts to get a more in-depth view of the exterior structure.

Not discovering anything out of the ordinary, he shifts his gaze to the pentagram configuration of waxy light circling them and chuckles. "I mean, that alone, partnered with the high rollin' theatrics, makes this whole shindig pretty bewildering. I'd say we are all being tricked here."

The sight of the cowboy trying to debunk the situation makes Cooper uneasy, and his gut tells him that the safety of using the bar as a barricade is inadequate. Abruptly, he stops his neurotic scrubbing and throws down his rag to the counter. He waits until the two men are distracted, and then, without making a scene, he rushes to the exit. As he reaches for the swinging wooden door panels, he realizes he is still wearing his work apron. Frantically, his shaky hands paw at the strings tied behind his back. While his fingers fiddle with freeing himself, he turns to shout to the others to announce his departure. "Sorry, Preacher, but my mind has changed like the wind, and I've decided I'm not stickin' around for the unpleasant festivities."

The moment he finishes his sentence, the knot unties, and he throws his apron to the floor beside him. Turning to the nearby pile of stacked tables blocking the window, he eyeballs his coat and runs to grab it from an upside-down table leg.

Still stunned, Preacher Boone lies on the floor, staring in disbelief at the bartender's change of plans. Not wanting to be left to fend for himself with only the cowboy for company, he springs to his feet to chase after him. When he sees the bartender grab his overcoat and head for the door, his pace switches to a sprint." Wait! I thought you were a man of your word. You told me you'd be here to help when the going gets tough!" he shouts.

The words ring true in Cooper's core, and a tinge of guilt travels through his veins. He feels the tension become unbearable, and he shrugs as he turns to face his friend. Unable to stomach confronting his look of desperation, he glances past his left shoulder and notices Alonzo playing with the candle's flame by squishing the wick between his fingers. His fear becomes overwhelming, and common sense takes over, freeing him from any notion of guilt he had felt.

As the confrontation continues by the exit, the cowboy, carried away with his investigation, remains unaware of the men's accumulating hostility. Captivated by the flame like a moth, he continues to play with the burning wick, holding it even closer than before to the brim of his hat. Oblivious to the turmoil his presence is causing, he licks his thumb and pointer finger to put out the flicker. "Sometimes, you just got to put these thingamabobs out and relight them to set them straight."

Both men slowly turn to glare at the idiocy happening across the room. As Alonzo pinches both fingers around the wick, a sizzling sound penetrates the tense air, fueling a smirk to form on his lips. Aberrant red smoke drifts into the air above as the flame smothers. Unbothered by the peculiar color, he chuckles at his accomplishment and turns his head to yell to the other end of the room. "What did I say? Oh, yeah, that I'm not someone you can shake a stick at," he says. Boastfully displaying his accomplishment, he holds the candle high and parades around the room.

The men near the exit are at a loss for words and stare flabbergasted at one another. Thinking the man, whom they believed to be a doofus, may be onto something, they cautiously take a few steps closer to observe the miracle.

Three steps into their journey, the black flame flickers and enthusiastically returns its demonic glow to the candlewick, stopping them dead in their tracks. Cooper takes a step backward to head for the door. "Like I was saying, Preacher, if you make it to the morning sun, I'll see y'all then. May the Lord be with you," he says.

Before the words process in Preacher Boone's ears, he hears the swinging doors *clack*, and the bartender is gone. Slowly pivoting on his feet to look at the exit brings anguish over his brow. He places his hand on his head to shield his straining eyes and prevent a tension headache from engulfing his mind.

Still living in his own little world, the cowhand holds the re-lit candle closer to his intrigued pupils. The unraveling events stump his mind, and for the first time, he is genuinely disconcerted by what he has just witnessed. He tries to hide his mounting terror over holding a candle that may be possessed, but his hands want nothing more than to get rid of it. Like carefully holding a hot potato, he tiptoes to set it back in the circle of wax he had plucked it from. "Well, that got me all balled up," he says with his finger pointing to the culprit.

He nervously laughs to break the confusing thoughts racing through his mind. Puzzled, he removes his hat and scratches his head. As he shifts his gaze to analyze the rest of the melting lineup one by one, each of the flames turns an ominous color of black, and the sight nearly causes him to jump out of his skin.

Slowly backing up to get away, he turns to the Preacher and takes a giant step, strategically positioning himself behind him to hide. "Oh, I see what you are trying to do. I know this game. You hired me here to try to hoodwink me and ruin my outstanding reputation."

Pointing to the pentagram, he hysterically laughs to cover his fear. "I'm still not buying whatever that is. You can't pull the wool over my eyes."

The accusation enrages Preacher Boone, and without hesitation, he turns to face his assailant. His skin has turned a shade of red that matches the wax on the floor. "How many times ought I have to tell you, boy?" His hands flail wildly above his shoulders to depict his annoyance.

At his wit's end, and with a nasty bout of anger, he locks out his elbow to point to the pentagram on the floor. "This is as real as the sunset outside. Why on God's green earth would I hire you otherwise? Do I appear to be a man who would willingly waste his money?"

Pacing back towards the bar, he throws his hands higher and releases a loud grunt. "Word of mouth was, you were the best paranormal Bronc Buster around," he says.

Alonzo falls silent in place, stunned by the newfound feisty diction leaving the meek man's lips. His eyes dart around the room as he tries to generate a way to lift the irritated man's spirits. Placing his hat back on top of his head, he opens his jaws in preparation to shout a sarcastic remark, but the Preacher, still on a mission, abruptly turns his body to continue berating him. "I mean, I've heard the tales of... of the haunted Concord!" he says. Taking a seat on a stool to brace his weak knees, he places his hands on his head to regain composure.

Hearing the words sparks a funny memory inside the cowboy's mind, and he clears his throat to knock off his laughter. Still wanting to be paid, Alonzo races to the Preacher's side to fend for the honor of his name and rebuild his credibility. "You heard about that, huh?" he asks.

Refraining from looking up, the Preacher moans to acknowledge the question and nods with his head still cupped in his hands.

Alonzo places his hand on the defeated man's shoulder and smirks as the memory carries his mind away to reminisce in glorified daydreams. "Boy, you sure are bringing back some flavorful memories. Honestly, I'm mighty tickled you learnt about that one."

Now, I'm about to address all my fellow buckaroos following along on this madhouse of a journey. Right about now, I reckon if I were you, I would be scratching my noggin, wondering what in the Hell we are talking about. Or you could ponder what in God's gravy the haunted Concord is, and why it tickles my hide with reminiscing memories.

First, let me make something clear: I consider that Preacher Boone and I have two very different recollections of the story. To be truthful with you, most everyone probably has a different account of what happened that night, not just him. Only me and one other person, maybe two, are party to the actual turn of events. The moment turned out to be sheer luck, and I happened to be at the right place at the right time.

After being injured from a roping incident I hate to talk about, I was out of work and pining for some means of survival. We all want to be rich; it's just finding the best way, or easiest, to buy the finer things in life. When the unique opportunity was put in front of me, I rode with it.

Rather than listening to me ramble, I will let you in on the story's honest-to-God truthful account. It would be nice not to keep this thumper penned up for once. The hell with it. This will be a hoot. It's about to be a wild ride, so saddle up, partners.

Four

Haunted Concord

1860, Jones Manor

G ray clouds toned in purple hues paint the sky as the sun hides behind the distant mountains to sleep. Light spurts of wind twist through the air, bringing vitality to a wind chime made of cascading silver cylinders hanging from the porch awning of a sizable manor. Every knocking dance of the blowing gale ruffles the small musical pieces of dangling silver and sounds a happy jingle.

The house stands as the largest in the small town's entirety. Well-maintained white pickets surround the outer perimeter of the ornate home. Its illuminated, partially open, shuttered windows allow light to be seen from a long distance down the torpid street. A series of polished silver sconces supply warm lighting both inside and out.

One room, specifically the parlor, exudes more luminosity than the others through a large plate-glass window. Inside the parlor room of the elaborate white-shingled manor, a wood fireplace blazes with a heap of coals, keeping everyone's skin within the four walls toasted to the touch. Along with the glow from the gleaming flames, a plethora of candelabras scatter the room in a non-selective decorative pattern, waiting in anticipation to supply light for a vital conversation. The lit wicks of their tall, skinny candles, made from wax resembling the color of a bee's honey, flicker like tiny torches, perfecting the quaint room's illumination.

Two velvet chairs with ornately embroidered stitching purposefully reside in front of the fireplace. A delicately carved end table made from dark cherry wood inhabits the space between the oversized armchairs. It provides a resting spot for an ornate sterling-silver candelabra and cut-crystal whiskey decanter set on a matching silver tray.

The tapers' warm flickers mirror in the pupils of a rugged man. Alonzo Bill is unrecognizable compared to his most recently discussed black leather and well-put-together image. In his prior days, before his calling, everyone he encountered deemed him rough around the edges. His camel-colored leather chaps, smudged with dirt from a ranch hand's long day of manual labor, validated that branding. All his leathers and suede appear a hair-off tone and haphazardly mixed. Matching his ensemble's bedraggled appearance, his chiseled face houses unkempt facial hair and grime smudges on his cheeks. The worse-for-wear cowboy hat on top of his head is an off-shade of white with patches of worn felt and a battered leather band embellishing the wide brim shading his dim eyes.

Entranced by the hypnotizing warmth from the fire, he sips on a cup of warm whiskey poured from the decanter and smirks. From his brief bout with luxury items, he knows he would do whatever it takes to make that moment his lifestyle.

Carved white painted wood molding frames the lovely fireplace. A woman's bustle bent over tending to the embers, reaches the high heavens as she uses a fire poker to rally the timber. Not only does the cowboy love the home's ambiance, but he also houses no shame in his idolization of the view. "Quite a nice place you got here, Jubilee."

Jubilee Jones stands upright to address her guest. As she turns to face Alonzo, the brilliance showcases her darkened beauty. Her black curls rest perfectly pinned in a formation on top of her head, with a few cascading past her ears. With each step taken by her petite laced boots, the artistically placed curls bounce. The pupils of her gentle eyes are captivating, with rich flecks of amber brown, and her cheeks' youthful rosy glow lightly shows through her cocoa complexion, displaying that she's shy of thirty. Jubilee adjusts the petticoat of her green satin dress, which is detailed with forest green velvet piping.

Her smitten feelings for the cowboy are as clear as day, and her lips exude a warm smile to speak. "That's mighty kind of you," she says as she glides to the empty armchair to sit.

As the fire picks up steam, Alonzo tilts the brim of his hat to shield his sensitive eyes and sunburnt skin from the heat of the blaze. His grimy hand clutches around the crystal cup. Lifting it to his mouth, he empties the rest of the contents into his throat and places the empty glass onto the end table between them.

Taking a deep breath, Jubilee closes her eyes to focus on inhaling an adequate amount of oxygen between the overly tightened strings of her corset. She determinedly curls the ends of her lips into a smile to mask the pain of her tortured ribs. As her eyelids open, she is met with the stern face of the ranch hand, and the view causes her foot to begin nervously tapping against the floor.

To help ease her angst, he reclines his posture and crosses his loose leg over his knee. Intertwining his fingers, he rests them on his lap and scans the attractive woman beside him. Regardless of his steadfast demeanor, her beauty overcomes him, and he gulps. "Now, I'm not here to dicker with you, Jubilee. I'm not a haggling kind of man."

Waiting for a sign of her concurrence, he opens a money pouch slung around his hip, pulls out a paper and pinch of tobacco, rolls it up, and rests it between his lips to light. As he fishes around inside the bag for his box of matches, he continues his thought, completely disregarding that she is about to reply. "Also, we should address the elephant in the room. It's no secret you are a hitched woman now. Regardless of your betrothed predicament, I am willing to help."

Unable to find the box, he leans over to a candle next to him to light his smoke. Taking a draw, his eyes slowly shift up to look at her, and for the first time, he acknowledges the worry on her face. "What seems to be the matter?"

Jubilee endeavors to calm herself by focusing on the therapeutic flames captive inside the fireplace's walls. Digging her soft fingers into the chair's stitching, she clears her throat. "I didn't realize how demanding my husband Sid's work hours were until after I moved in on the wedding night. I understand his commitment to him being the sheriff' n' all. Regardless of my mustered feelings, he takes my words as nagging. He's not too accommodating when the evenings get unbearable. I'm just left so many a night by my Lil' lonesome..." Her yammering wears on the cowboy's tired ears, and with his roll-up still in hand, he nods off. As his chin pitches forward to his clavicle, the brim of his hat hits the bridge of his nose and jars him awake. Scrambling to adjust his seated position, his foot startles, and the shifted weight of his heel causes the floorboard to creak under his spur.

Alonzo takes another drag of his calming stick to disassociate himself from the jarring sound, but Jubilee jumps in her seat and frantically scans her surroundings for the culprit. Her skin turns pale with terror, and her eyes widen with fear. When she cannot immediately identify the cause, her mind races, and her hands wrap tightly around the arms of the chair for stability.

The ranch hand notices her dramatic reaction, lifts his hand to take the blame, and chuckles. "Sorry, darlin', my foot just has a mind of its own sometimes," he says as he extends his boot into the air and shakes his leg. As he shrugs his shoulders to diffuse the situation, he takes another drag off his cigarette.

Noticing she is still a bundle of nerves, he changes his approach and silences his laughter. "I know that was awful snake-headed of me. Please, continue."

Her pupils glare daggers into his soul. Annoyed that he is not taking the situation seriously, she rolls her eyes and straightens her posture. "As I was saying, when left alone, I've heard some dreadful noises coming from our carriage outside... I reckon it could be a ghost of some sort, and on account, Sid might think I'm as crazy as a loon, so I don't dare tell him," she says.

Though deep down, he thinks she is crazier than a church bell, he nods in agreement to validate her concerns. Pretending to get stirred up, he springs to his feet and beelines it to the fireplace to dispose of his cigarette butt. Looking at the intricate carvings surrounding the open flames, he pretends to ponder. "Sounds like you have quite the predicament there." He paces the length of the room as if devising a plan.

She is desperate to hear any potential solution to remedy her dilemma, no matter how crazy it may be. Jubilee intently shifts her body to the edge of her seat to wait for a miracle. Her head turns to follow every lap he takes, and each hypothesizing huff from his mouth teases her excited mind.

The cowhand senses her admiring eyes watching his every move, and he plays into her ethos-fueled hunger. With a flick of his wrist to the ceiling, his body abruptly turns toward her. "I tell you what: You said the ghostly noise happens around what hour? When the sky falls dark?" He stares at her with curiosity.

Overjoyed to help solve the mystery, she quickly tilts her body to glance at a tall grandfather clock steadfastly ticking in the room's corner. The lids of her eyes squint around her pupils as she attempts to read the time through the dim lighting. "Anytime now," she says.

Knowing people's fears emerge when night falls over the sky, Alonzo recognizes that the timing is ideal for drawing her into his money-making ploy. Enthused by her sense of urgency to solve the terrifying mystery, he relishes the lucrative opportunity. Flinging his hand to his chin as if dramatically pondering, a rush of adrenaline makes his body twitch and jump with excitement. "Well, that there is some Hell-fired timing!"

His elated tone imparts a sense of security that her problems will soon resolve. As she leans forward in her seat, her lips grin, and she touches her hand to her heart. "So, that means you'll help?" she asks.

His lips squinch into a contradicting face as he hoists his palm into the air to signal her to slow down. "Whoa, little lady, not so fast. I reckon I can fancy you with a fair deal for my time, if you want my services." Noticing her nod, he continues, "I will inspect the haunted carriage, and for the price, if I find any spookiness, I will rid you of it for a small fee."

Unable to contain her eagerness, she leaps to her feet to answer him. Each word flows from her lips a mile per minute as she grovels. "We will pay anything. Sid will be more than willing to pay whatever the price is for my safekeeping."

Alonzo ceases all movement to peer into the center of her pleading corneas and smirks. "Looks like we have ourselves a fine little deal, then," he says. His smile grows friendlier, stretching from ear to ear as he extends his hand toward her to secure the verbal contract with a shake.

Before his elbow can lock, Jubilee's outreaching arm invades his personal space. As their hands grasp together to seal the deal, a shrill screeching noise echoes from the carriage parked outside. She freezes, and her fingers tremble with fear. The sound has a haunting pull on her ears. Swiftly retracting her hand to stabilize her distress, she nervously paces the room's perimeter. "Did you hear that? That means it's happening. You have my and Sid's word, I swear. Now, please, skeet before it's too late to catch it!" Her clamoring hand motions to the window facing the direction of the carriage below.

Loving a good fight, Alonzo lightly wraps his hand around the cold ivory handle of the Colt revolver positioned in the worn holster on his hip. Upon taking a few steps towards the door, he pauses and turns to take a last glimpse of her exuberant face. Caught up in the emotion of heading to fight an unknown battle, he quickly taps his finger against his left cheek and leans his head in her direction. "Do I at least get a kiss for luck?" he flirtatiously smirks.

Hearing his solicitation initially makes her blush, but her excitement quickly becomes annoyance as the awful idea of touching her lips to the cowboy's dirty face sinks in. She rolls her eyes and sternly points toward the door. "You're a real ten-cent man, you know that?" she says.

Alonzo takes her words as a compliment, encouraging him to part his lips to spout a new advance. Before he can get another word out, Jubilee's harsh stare and her motioning wrist toward the front door immediately silence him. "Just go!" Her sharp tone rings throughout the room.

Her rebuff surprises Alonzo, as he is not used to a woman rejecting him. To cover his hide from the humiliation, he plays off his advance as a joke and sarcastically throws his hands into the sky, playfully accepting her dismissal. "Damn, girl, you didn't have to make up your mind so quickly. That's fine. I can respect that. I'm good as gone," he says with a chuckle.

His fingers pull the makings of another cigarette from his money pouch, and he rolls it up. Placing it lightly between his lips, he leans over a burning candle next to the front door and lights it. As he inhales a deep breath of nicotine, his nerves calm, and he exits the home.

The street outside of the manor is dead-silent. Even the breeze doesn't release a peep as it brushes his exposed face. Something feels off to Alonzo, and he can't place a finger on the root cause of his internal turmoil.

As he takes a few more steps into the surrounding nightfall, he flinches and stops his advance, surprised by the sound of a scurrying mouse crossing his path. His dilated pupils fixate on the tiny rodent, and he shakes his head and chuckles. Immediately, he mocks the situation to compensate for the underlying fear stirring in the pit of his stomach. "Beef-headed woman. Ghosts don't exist," he says.

Turning his body to take one last glimpse at the house, he observes Jubilee's nervous face peering out the window. Without a second thought, he lifts his hand to give a single wave and smirks with the cigarette resting between his lips. She anxiously waves back, and he continues his lightless walk to the ominous carriage.

As he closes in on the horse-drawn coach, his eyes shift to analyze the outer structure for a cause of the creaking sounds. At a closer look, he realizes that the stationary body is slightly swaying on its own. The sight fills his mind with doubts and makes him question his original assumption that the woman is crazy. With only an arm's length between him and a possible haunted encounter, he swallows a large gulp of air and squashes the cigarette butt under the toe of his boot. "Well, money has been slim pickings lately, so here goes nothing."

Not wanting the snoopy woman to judge his handiwork from the window, he walks to the carriage entrance on the opposite side, away from the house's view. Placing one hand on his holstered gun, he wraps the fingers of the other around the cold metal handle, closes his eyes to pray, and quickly swings the door open mid-Amen.

A gust of wind exits the inside of the carriage and hits his closed eyelids, and he quickly draws his revolver. Blindly pointing the gun barrel toward the open door and expecting the worst, he discovers playful laughter rather than ghostly shrieks. His eyes spring open. Swiftly, he lowers his firearm back to the holster and silently gloats through the opening in disbelief.

Inside the lavish compartment are red-velvet upholstered accents covering the ceiling and inside door panels, unique cowhide benches on opposite ends facing one another, and muted gray paisley-patterned wallpaper. Sitting, slumped on the bench closest to the back of the caboose is a relaxed clean-cut man wearing a sheriff's badge, with his freshly starched cream-colored shirt partially unbuttoned. His hair is chestnut brown and matches his enthralled pupils. The lack of silvered locks places his age shy of forty. He appears to be having the time of his life with a blonde-haired woman in her mid-twenties, straddling him, wearing a ruffled pink satin dress hiked to her hips.

Engulfed in the heat of passion and oblivious to the ghost hunter's presence, they continue insatiably kissing each other as Alonzo quietly relishes the moment. "Whoa-ho-ho," he says with a laugh. Swiftly, he scans over his right and left shoulder to make sure there are no witnesses, then hotfoots it into the carriage.

As he gently shuts the door behind him, he clears his throat to gain the lovebirds' attention. "I reckon this is where the shindigs are," he says. Taking a seat across from them, he makes himself comfortable. "Leaping lizards was it chilly out there!" he says with a shiver.

The man, realizing he is in trouble, tries to divest himself of his affiliation and pushes the woman from his lap onto the floor. While attempting to catch his breath, he frantically acknowledges Alonzo. "Who in the Sam Hill are you?" he asks as they stare wide-eyed at Alonzo.

Entertained by their flabbergasted expression, Alonzo takes time to formulate his response, and, after a minute or two, he opens his mouth to speak. "That's right! You don't know me, but I sure have heard a mess of talk about you by God."

Still confused by the boisterous encounter, they sit silently leering at the cowboy. Trying to pinpoint the cause of their puzzled expressions, he scans his outfit to see if he has something out of place, and, realizing they haven't officially met, he wipes his dirty hand on his dusty suede chaps and prepares for a formal introduction. "Good Lord, where are my manners?" he says as he extends his hand toward the man.

The woman sitting on the floor appears dumbfounded and remains at a loss for words. She glances at her lover, and his expression reads the same. Impatient with the snail's pace of the Sheriff's tentatively extending hand, Alonzo assuredly leans forward and tightly clutches his fingers to shake. Taking the lead, he confidently finishes his introduction. "Pleased to make your acquaintance, Sheriff. I'm Alonzo. Alonzo Bill," he says with a smile.

Still stunned by the cowboy's intrusion and forceful shaking of his hand, he quietly stutters. "My name--"

Hearing the nerves fluttering through his voice, Alonzo puts the man out of his misery and cuts off his speech. "No need to go through the trouble. I know who you are, Sid," he says.

As he confidently hovers above the situation's awkwardness, he rummages through his coin pouch for the makings of another cigarette. He places the rolled tobacco between the corner of his lips. Patting his pockets, he remembers he doesn't have a way to light it and glances up at the Sheriff. "You got a match?" he asks.

The man slowly pulls a matchstick from his uniform pocket and leans forward to hand it to Alonzo. Giving a quick nod of thanks, he grins and snatches the match, using the side wallpaper as a point of friction to ignite the flame. Shielding the end of the tobacco stick with his hand, he uses the other to light the tip while inhaling a deep breath. As his lungs exhale a giant puff of smoke into the passenger's faces, he lets out a dramatic sigh and then leans back, relaxing in his seat to tell a story.

"You two wouldn't believe the day I've been having. I was approaching this here carriage thinking there would be a ghost waiting inside, when it's just another case of an unhappy partner cheatin'," he says. Basking in the silence, he chuckles to himself and rests the back of his head against the seat, tilting it to look up at the ceiling. He takes another drag to settle the last bit of his leftover anxiety and blows the cloud of smoke into the air.

Knowing there is little he can do to reverse the scenario, Sid settles into the situation. Realizing the petite woman is still on the floor, he helps her onto the seat next to him, and they both stare at the cowhand with skepticism. The woman, no longer able to hold her tongue, tugs on her partner's sleeve. "Why are you here?" she asks.

Her inquisitive words snap Sid out of his confused trance, and he redirects her question to Alonzo. "Yeah, what she said," he says.

Feeding into the mystery, he slowly straightens his posture to sit up and stare at them. His upper body leans forward as if getting ready to disclose a secret, and he winks at the dame. "Always got to hand it to the painted ladies of the world for keeping us men on track," he says.

His vulgarity disgusts her, and she presses her nose in the air to snub him. Alonzo Bill snickers at the prissy response and redirects his attention to Sid. "Your wife hired me to investigate a *haunted carriage out back* that kept making spooky sounds each night while her beloved husband was away, riskin' his life doing his civil duties."

Seeing his words have piqued the couple's interest, he leans closer and takes a drag. "Isn't it funny, Sheriff? Here she thought the ruckus was a ghost when you were out here knocking boots with that one there."

The woman glares at her companion as his complexion turns an unnatural shade of white, and he nervously swallows. Trying to secure her alibi as a naïve, fun-loving girl, she changes her lustful demeanor and pushes Sid away. She raises the pitch of her voice to portray a virtuous woman who finds offense in the situation and, with a look of shock, she aggressively slaps his shoulder. "Golly gee, Sid! You didn't tell me you were a taken man!" she says.

Knowing he's instigated turmoil, Alonzo smugly sits back in his seat to watch the conflict unfold. Unable to take another moment of not adding fuel to the fire, he points his cigarette at the upset woman and chimes in. "I reckon I know your type, darlin'. In my days as a respectable buckaroo, we would call you a buckle bunny."

His insulting words strike a nerve to her core, and the facade of innocence momentarily drops from her face. With the realization of her fake persona's exposure, she indignantly sits up in her seat, straightens her dress, and regains composure. She clears her throat to draw attention away from her shifting mood. "Whatever do you mean?" she asks.

The cowboy sees right through her fake presentation and laughs. "Don't act silly with me, girl."

His words miff her, and she lets out a loud gasp to show her contempt. Ignoring the drama, he puts his burning cigarette out on the seat bolster and reaches into his pouch to retrieve ingredients for two fresh ones. After placing one in his mouth, he lengthens his arm to pass the other to a speechless Sid. "I reckon you'll need this after the words I'm about to unload," he says.

Before accepting the smoke, Sid glances at the woman sitting next to him and, avoiding her gaze, reluctantly nods. Still processing the root cause of the encounter, he complacently takes out a new match from the box in his pocket and lights both of their cigarettes.

The cowboy sucks in a whiff of nicotine-laced smoke, and his hand waves in the air to gesture for the others to listen. "Believe it or not, I was a cowboy once, and with that title comes women slinging responsibilities," he says with a shrug. Pointing the smoking stick towards the woman's displeased face, he continues. "Buckle bunnies were what we called the tramps we could lie down each night."

Sid proudly adjusts his badge and buttons his shirt before chuckling. "You're making me feel more and more like I'm in the wrong career," he says. Refraining from looking directly at his lady of the night, he glimpses her out of his peripherals as she angrily crosses her arms and pouts for attention.

She clenches her back molars as she tries to fight off her boiling anger. Finally, unable to hold her tongue a moment longer, she says, "My name is not buckle bunny; it's Shirley."

Alonzo Bill ignores her interruption and laughs at the sheriff's remark. Shrugging, he turns toward her and takes a moment to analyze each pinched feature of her soured face. "Shirley, Shirley, Shirley," he says as he ponders. As he takes a drag, he flicks ash onto the carpet. "What's the latter part of that name?" he asks.

Irritated, she crosses her arms and turns away to look out the window to answer. "Thompson," she says. Her willingness to cooperate excites the cowman, and her answer flips a switch in his mind, lighting his eyes with an epiphany.

Scanning each of their faces, Sid pauses, directing his focus solely on Alonzo's newfound excitement. Quickly, he becomes impatient with his silence and jumps the gun to inquire about the cause. "What's that look for?" he asks.

The inquiry knocks the ranch hand away from his reminiscing, and he starts laughing hysterically. "Shirley Thompson, I am such a dadgum fool. Here

I was sitting across from you, thinking you looked mighty familiar, when, in fact..."

Worrying he may have dirt on her, she irritably grunts, interrupting his train of thoughts. Unable to stand another minute of his harassment, she gathers all her belongings and loudly interjects. "You are ... you are disgusting, and make me mad as Hell, Mr. Alonzo Bill. Sid, I'm not doing this anymore. I'm leaving!"

Without waiting for a plea to stay from her beau, she shifts her weight and exits the carriage through the same door Alonzo had entered. Sid watches the exit in disbelief and laughs as the door slams behind her. "You sure know how to win over the ladies," he says.

The cowboy smirks at his quick wit. "I reckon that little lady was just in an all-horns-and-rattles mood. On a good day, I'm a real ace in the hole when it comes to wooing," he says as he puts his cigarette out by twisting it into the seat.

His companion glowers at Alonzo's slovenly behavior with disgust. While maintaining his glare of frustration at the dirty ranch hand, he purposely reaches over and tamps out the last remains of his burning butt in a copper ashtray on the seat next to Alonzo. "You got to stop doing that, cowpoke. You know you got an ash-hopper right next to you," he says. As he falls back into his seat to unload his stress, his lips smirk at the feeling of the rich upholstery under his fingertips. "These here seats are made from custom hides from Tahoe's finest cattle. They told me they were the only ones like this for miles. One of a kind."

The cowboy bypasses Sid's speech regarding his admiration for the finer things in life and switches the subject to what he finds most interesting. He has a plan at hand, and does not want to miss seizing the opportunity to execute it while his compadre is in a gleeful mood. Clearing his throat, he sits up slightly in his seat and warmly laughs. "Yessiree, that's great. I'd say we are amigos now. Wouldn't you say that too, Sid?"

Sid casually shrugs. "Whoa, there, Bronc Buster. You ran my lady out of this here carryall. If I have any say so, that is not a quality of friendship that I seek."

Alonzo, not keen on his response, sits taller in his seat in preparation to persuade him to reconsider. "True, but you gotta remember, you are not exactly a bachelor, Sheriff," he says, gesturing with his hands. Sitting up straighter, he shifts his glance and motions to the carriage's window. "If my recollection is correct, you are legally betrothed to that fine piece of calico just inside those doors."

Watching the cowboy peek out the gathered shams of the carriage window causes Sid to become restless. Worried his wife will see him peering in the house's direction, he dramatically waves his hands to get Alonzo to retreat from the window, but gets the opposite reaction he had hoped for. Rather than sit back, he moves closer and opens the curtains further.

Sid spots the face of Jubilee nervously looking out the parlor's picture window in their direction. Quickly, he hops out of his seat and, with the speed of a striking snake, hits Alonzo's fingers away from the curtains and out of sight. "Are you trying to crawl my hump, cowboy?" he asks as a bead of sweat drips from his brow.

The defensive reaction proves his care for his wife and how far he will go to keep peace within the four walls of their home. Alonzo grins and retracts from the window while holding his hands above his head to show his innocent intentions. "It sure would be a shame if that sweet, wholesome sage hen sitting in her warm surroundings found out that her only true love has been nothing but a twister of the truth."

Allowing his back to rest heavily against the seat, he makes himself comfortable, stretching his legs until his boots rest on the seat next to Sid. "Wouldn't it, Sheriff?" he asks.

Immediately, Sid's mind connects the dots and realizes the cowhand poses a threat. He sits back without a word leaking from his lips, and his eyes fill with remorse over the carelessness of his indiscretion.

Resolute in his mission to make a financial gain, Alonzo shakes his head in disapproval, prepared to turn the knife of shame further into the lifeless flesh of the cheating husband. "I reckon you two would be the talk of the whole town," he says as he leans forward and pats his knee.

The condescending tone of the threat rubs the Sheriff the wrong way, and his face becomes red with anger. Swiftly, he shakes his head and extends his palm flat in the air. "Whoa, now, partner. I hope you aren't trying to bulldoze me into doing something I don't want to," he says, awkwardly chuckling to lessen the severity of the situation.

The words bring forth an understanding stare from the cowboy, and for a moment, he scans the ceiling to gather his thoughts. Lowering his chin, he strokes the hair on his jawline. "I wouldn't say bulldozing is the right word. More like a friend just trying to help another get back in apple-pie order with the missus."

Ultimately shifting his approach, he softens the expressions on his face to compliment the man and coax him to agree. "We both know you are a man of honesty," he says.

Sid eagerly eats up every word falling from Alonzo's lips and, in a daze, nods to show approval. Adjusting his posture in his seat, he puffs out his chest to show resolution. "I sure am," he says.

Observing his actions, Alonzo knows he has the Sheriff right where he wants him, and proceeds to stroke his ego. As he ramps up his energy, he tries to rally the badged man's ethos and make him dependent on his words of affirmation. His eyes look out the window to give the anxious man space to think. "I take it you aren't the stealing type neither, then," he says. When his words finish, his head remains looking out the window as he uses his peripheral vision to watch his response.

Sid polishes the star-shaped Sheriff's badge fastened to his uniform shirt pocket and smiles while reminiscing over his power. "You're right. I have this here badge for a reason, cowboy."

Tilting his vision back to the lamenting public servant, Alonzo lifts his fingers and salutes him in agreement. "I know because you are a good man, Sheriff," he says, then takes a brief pause. His smile grows more expansive with each word of praise. Lifting his hand to the sky to signal he has had an epiphany, he speaks, encouraging validation of his opinion. "Any God fearin' person wouldn't go to the saloon and drink without paying the ole bar dog, would they?" he asks.

Immediately, Sid gets a visual of someone in his town stealing from an honest business owner who is just trying to earn a living and put food on the table for their family. Suddenly, his swirling thoughts halt, and his pupils raise to look at Alonzo. "Come on, now, where are you going with this? Get a wiggle on before I take the big jump," he says.

Portraying the role of a captured perpetrator, Alonzo throws both of his hands up in the air as if admitting to the crime. "All right, you caught me, Sheriff. Sometimes, my words get away from me when I get going with my wobbling jaw. What I'm trying to say is, like with anything, my service comes at a price." He stares across the bench in silence, his hands still raised.

Unable to contain his nerves surrounding what may happen next, the lawman appears composed and reluctantly parts his lips to speak. "My ears are open," he says.

Before carrying on with the rest of his statement, the cowboy takes his inquiry as success and sprawls his arms across the carriage to slap his knee. "Well, if this isn't a hog-killing time, then I don't know what is," he says. Retreating backward to his seat, he hunches his spine forward, leaning toward the sheriff, and wrenches his hands together to talk business.

"Lucky for you, I'm in a generous mood today, so I'm willing to be a dickering man." Motioning with his hands and taking no pause for negotiation, he continues. "A few silver dollars, and I will be out of your hair in the wink of an eye." Believing he's offered a reasonable price, he wastes no time extending his hand forward to shake on it.

The sight of the ranch hand's palm creeping closer to seal the deal makes Sid's mind run wild with opportunities. Rather than being pushed into a submissive corner of shame, he contemplates ways he, too, can benefit from the shyster's plan. Just as he is about to cave, he pulls his hand back from the grip and holds up his pointer finger to signal the other party to wait. His eyes light up with excitement over a brilliant idea, and words run from his mouth a mile a minute. "I reckon I might just have a surefire idea that will make us both hit pay dirt."

The solicitation intrigues Alonzo Bill, and though skeptical, he is open to listening. "All right, Sheriff. I'm all into fining one's flint, so shoot."

Meeting the cowman halfway, Sid leans forward and lowers the volume of his voice as he attempts to con the con. His hands wave in the air to show enthusiasm, and his mouth spews compliments to stroke his ego. "In all my years of being sheriff of this here town, I've met no one who could run their tongue quite as well as you did just now."

As the words of admiration ring through his ears, Alonzo takes the bait and tips the felt brim of his hat in agreement. Bending closer to the source of affirmation, he circles his hand in the air, signaling Sid to keep them coming. "I'd be lying if I said I wasn't flattered," he says.

Not wanting to lose the brilliant train of thoughts flowing like a river from his conniving mind, Sid stops him from fishing for compliments by holding up a finger to silence him. To make sure no one is eavesdropping, his head nervously tilts towards the window to listen for any unusual noises coming from outside the stationary carriage. He hurries the pace of his voice. "Now, you said my wife solicited you to rid this here carriage of ghosts."

Looking back at the eager eyes staring at him makes Sid question how she even believed Alonzo qualified to perform any job, especially one requiring such a specific skill set. For a split second, his mind jumps to the thought of his betrothed going behind his back and paying someone for a service and it heats his blood. Trying to calm his spiraling thoughts, he closes his eyes. "Now, why she chose an eyeballer like you for the job beats me," he says with a chuckle.

Still basking in the fuzzy warmth provided by the compliment, Alonzo carelessly shrugs off the passive remark, and he attributes the dig solely to the man's jealousy over his wife being behind closed doors with another man. "That's a fair question," he says with a grin. Shifting his weight back in his seat, he chuckles as his posture relaxes.

Sid scoots to the edge of the bench to get closer. "What would you say if I told you I could get you more jobs just like this one, and all you'd have to do is show up and collect the cash?"

Alonzo surveys the rough calluses on his hand from the intensive manual labor he had to endure roping cattle, and the idea of making more money with no physical work entices him. Placing his hand lightly on his chin, he ponders a life of riches with no sweat dripping off his forehead, then motions for his potential business partner to continue his explanation.

Ready and willing to divulge the details of the scheme, Sid's pupils light up with the thought of extra cash, and his voice grows louder with excitement. "As Sheriff of this town, I know we have a lot of cracked churchgoers that believe just about anything the converter tells them. Now, if I gave you a brand-spanking-new title and solicited you as the town's only mystery-solving ghost hunter..."

His eyes analyze his audience's reaction for signs of receptiveness and scan for any inkling of hesitation. He switches his speech to move even faster. "If I used my hog at the trough words to tell a few tall tales, it would blow you out of the Mississippi river with work!" He throws his hands into the air to show his excitement and to get Alonzo rallied up.

The relaxed cowboy calmly analyzes the gaping smile. "What's in it for you?" he asks.

Without giving a moment of pause, the Sheriff confidently answers with a simple shrug. "Nothing major. Just a sliver of the coins from each of your earnings, no time in the calaboose, and assisting me in keeping the left-handed wife dry," he says.

Before allowing the ranch hand to respond, he sticks his hand to shake on the deal. "What you say, cowboy? Are we in cahoots?" he asks.

Still reclining back in his seat, Alonzo squints at the extended hand before him and crosses his arms to think. As a bead of sweat slowly rolls down Sid's brow, he springs up in his seat and smiles. "I can sit with that," he says. Tightly wrapping his grip around the waiting hand, he enthusiastically shakes on the deal. With each movement of their hands, he imagines dollar signs floating in the surrounding air.

The Sheriff smiles back. "Cheers to the start of a beautiful partnership, and more money than we will know what to do with," he says.

Five

A Little Corral Dust Never Hurt Anyone

The screech of the carriage door wildly swinging open causes both men to jump and retract back into their respectful seats at lightning speed. As they look into the darkness and brace themselves for the unknown, that shadowy outline of a woman holding a fire poker emerges, standing still in the doorway, her grip tight around the handle.

She clasps her chest with her free hand to steady her gasping breath. Stepping closer, she peers inside, giving the men a glimpse of her face.

They stare in silence at Jubilee Jones's frightening demeanor and refrain from moving a single inch so as not to stir up trouble or put any unnecessary ideas in her head.

The sight of the familiar men causes her grip on the makeshift weapon to loosen and her posture to relax. "Bless my soul! I thought my poor little heart would jump right out of my chest," she says as the hand holding her chest extends to motion that she needs a moment to regain her composure.

After slowing her hyperventilating, she scans the cabin's interior while regaining her bearings. The sight of her husband confuses her, and she points at him with the sharp end of the fire poker. "Wait... Sid? Aren't you supposed to be Sheriffing right now?" she asks.

Sid gulps at the sight of the sharpened end of the weapon. His nerves create a stammer in his speech as tiny beads of sweat appear in the divots of the scrunching skin on his forehead. He is at a loss for words.

The severity of his quivering puts Alonzo on the edge of his seat. Concerned by how his new business partner appears to be dealing with a high-pressure situation, he takes matters into his own hands. Attempting to avoid the possibility of the sheriff blowing their negotiated arrangement, he jumps out of his seat and slaps his hand against Sid's back. "He sure was, Jubilee. Isn't that right, Sid?"

Sid's eyes wince from the painful sting lingering from the whack, and his head frantically shakes in agreement. "Yup, that's right," he says.

Still pointing her spear-like poker in his direction, Jubilee scrutinizes her husband. Using his sleeve, he wipes sweat from his brow to prevent it from dripping into his eyes. Her eyes squint with skepticism as she further analyzes the questionable situation.

Alonzo Bill fixates on her apprehensive expression and reads between the lines. He can tell she is not buying the narrative. Scanning the confining walls of the coach, he racks his brain to muster the right combination of words to ease the building tension. "Got to hand it to you, Jubilee--you caught us. Your sweet husband was not at work. That doting man sitting next to me was coming home early to surprise your pretty little self with flowers when he heard a commotion coming from this here carriage!" he says as his hands dramatically flail with his words. As he analyzes the room's receptiveness to his testimony, he catches the sight of Sid's face, paralyzed with foreboding.

Jubilee glares at her betrothed's paling appearance and is unconvinced by the doting story. Trying to knock him out of the peculiar trance-like state, she ambles onto the top carriage step, reaches inside, and flails her hand in front of him to gain his attention. Unable to evoke a response, she continues her hand's motion while addressing the cowboy. "Has he gone off his rocker? What's wrong with him? Did he see a ghost or something?" she questions.

Alonzo feeds off her notion to protect the secret of their manly partnership. "Those are some good questions you have, Jubilee. You sure are one smart hen. Yes, he saw a ghost," he says.

Scanning the carriage in a frenzy, her eyes expand with fear. "He did?" she asks.

The cowboy allows her mind a minute to run wild before interrupting her thoughts. "Well, we both did."

No longer able to hold her tongue, Jubilee spouts a string of questions that annoys Alonzo. "If you let me finish my story, you would find out what scared the living daylights out of your dear husband and spurred him to have that poker-face."

As Jubilee listens closely, he watches her demeanor soften. Seizing the opportunity, Alonzo jumps from his seat to assist her inside. "Let me help you up here to sit. I reckon you might prefer sitting for the news I'm about to unleash upon your ears," he says as he offers his hand.

Still fixated on the fire poker in her grasp, Sid's eyes refrain from blinking. He is petrified.

Jubilee's eyes rapidly glance at her husband's stock-still face for approval, and his unresponsiveness offers no answer. Looking back to the cowboy, she takes matters into her own hands and accepts the gentleman's courtesy.

Alonzo notes the Sheriff's anxious glare at the pointed metal object and quickly brainstorms an idea to remedy the situation. Distracted by the fear of tripping over her floor-length dress, Jubilee gathers it as well as possible while still maintaining a handhold on the poker. As she ascends the last step, Alonzo extends his free hand to collect the trifling weapon. "First and foremost, a lady, especially one as eye-catching as a speckled stallion, should never have to bear the mighty burden of holding a weapon as dangerous as the one in your pretty little hand," he says. Wiggling the fingers on his waiting hand grabs her attention.

She smiles with embarrassment, and her cheeks turn a bright shade of red. "Of course! Silly me, I almost forgot about it," she says. Trying to play off the awkward situation as a joke, she swings the poker like a dueling sword, and her husband flinches.

The cowboy's eyes follow the swaying stick like a hypnotic pendulum. Intercepting the object, he snatches it mid-swing, and she steps to the far side of the cabin and sits next to her betrothed. Once she's settled, Alonzo carefully sets the iron stick beside him and stares at the two lovebirds. He clears his throat to get her undivided attention. "So, Jubilee, as I was saying, your sweet," he says as he leans and slaps Sid's knee, "sweet husband sitting next to you detected a fearsome tussle inside this here coach, from outside the door right there."

Alonzo dramatically points to the door to gather suspense and watches as she shifts her focus to where he is pointing. "In the blink of an eye, he flung open the door with his pistol drawn, willing to die standing up for you. Jubilee, all I can say is, your husband is one brave son of a gun."

Sensing the love of the man sitting next to her warms her heart. She lovingly places her hand on his knee to show her undying appreciation. Slowly, she turns her face to look into his glossed-over eyes. "What a brave soul," she says.

The boastful admiration for her husband causes Alonzo Bill's imagination to replay the actual series of events that transpired, but he refrains from letting a chuckle leave his lips and remains amused by his convincing ability. "He sure is Jubilee. What I am about to say will shock the daylights out of you."

Clearing his throat, he sits up straighter in his seat. "So, there he was, standing right outside the door with his shooting iron in one hand and your freshly picked flowers in the other, ready to fight for your honor... then, suddenly, he notices me grappling with the ghost! The same one you've heard late at night," he says dramatically.

Watching his hand wave around, reenacting the fight with a spirit, causes her eyes to grow wide with shock. She cannot fathom proving everyone wrong about her ethereal concerns, and stammers at the thought of being somewhere truly haunted. Her body is frozen in place as her eyes slowly scan the surrounding space. "So, I-I was right? There was a ghost?" she asks.

Hearing her fear-driven stutter causes the cowboy to turn in her direction. He knows he has her exactly where he wants her. Trying to match her genuine terror, he forces his face to remain expressionless as he nods in agreement. "You were right all along about the ghost, Jubilee, and boy, oh, boy, was it the nastiest ghost I ever have seen."

His imagination-provoking words plant a seed in her mind, and as her thoughts flourish, she attempts to distract herself. Swiveling her body, she observes the man sitting beside her and analyzes his trembling hands. Unwilling to be engulfed by the terror, her diverted mind searches for holes in the narrative. "What happened to the flowers?" she asks.

Before she has enough time to form a hypothesis, Alonzo steps in and lifts his hand to silence her. "After everything this poor man has been through, saving you from specters and all, that's what you are pining over? A handful of daisies?" he asks.

She takes his inquisition as a jab directed toward her devotion to her husband's health and safety. Her interrogating stare shifts back to Alonzo, and her building angry energy pierces the stillness. He attempts to squelch her rage by embellishing the story further. "Whoa, there, little lady. I reckon I'm about to get there if you just let me finish the story."

Clearing his throat, he continues creating the wild narrative. His presentation becomes painfully slow as he tries to bide his time to muster up what will happen next to the duo. Ready to carry on, he transitions his hushing hand to a lowered, tightened fist, believing the posture better matches a look of stirred-up emotion. "Now, this time, I'm going to finish," he says.

Pointing to the man sitting beside her, he raises his voice louder. "Your brave husband, the Sheriff, witnessed me battling the ghost with my bare hands. I told him to run, but instead of cowering, he climbed right up in this carriage and fought with everything he could muster."

He looks down at Sid and shakes his head in solace. "That God-darn ghost didn't stand a fighting chance to win against a man so Hell-bent on protecting his woman."

His storyline hooks her, and it comforts her to know that she has a hero sitting next to her. She scoots closer and places her hand on the catatonic man's thigh.

Alonzo Bill motions the sign of the cross into the air and peers up to the ceiling to pay homage. "Thank the Lord, we won the battle with no skin off our backs, but your flowers were, sadly, a casualty. That thieving ghost ripped them straight from his manly gripping hand and took them back into its mysterious world. The ghost and flowers were gone in a single poof, like a sideshow magician's magic trick." With an air of sadness for losing her gift, he looks to the floor to feed her guilt.

Amazed by the bravery of the men, she moves her face closer to look Sid straight in the eyes, as if trying to thank him telepathically. When it doesn't provoke any response, she speaks to engage him in the conversation. "Is that true, Sid?"

The cowhand peers at the man being questioned, waiting with her for a response. Believing too much time has passed with no answer after her query, he becomes nervous that the Sheriff will spoil the tedious footwork laid to convince the skeptical woman. Seeing her eyes questioningly squint at her husband's disturbed state, Alonzo inconspicuously nudges his boot with an aggressive kick, inciting him to talk.

The pain of his toe being stubbed shoots through the nerves in Sid's leg, and his face scrunches with a wince. "By Harry!" he shouts. His teeth clench as he reaches down to rub his foot. Realizing his reaction may appear suspicious, he adjusts to pretend he is polishing his shoe's leather. His angry pupils dart to the cowboy, who's sitting silently with a shit-eating grin plastered across his face.

"Every last word of it's true, Jubilee," Sid says. Slowly straightening his posture, he turns to his wife, lightly places his hand on top of hers, and gazes deeply into her eyes. "I would do anything for my woman."

Overjoyed by his devotional words, she leans towards him and kisses his cheek. As her lips touch his skin, his jaw muscles relax, and he smirks in disbelief over the low-down cowboy saving his cheating hide. "You sure did a fine job finding that fellow sitting there, Jubilee. He got the job done, lickety-split, and rid our lives of that ghost for good. Got to hand it to you, sugar--you have hired the best mystery fighter I have ever seen."

The ranch hand shrugs and chuckles while tipping his hat at the couple. "It's all in a day's work." While silently reminiscing on his days as a free-roaming cowboy, he says, "Believe me, I've experienced some crazier..."

Paying no attention to the start of his trailing storyline, the newlyweds stare into each other's eyes and begin wildly kissing as Alonzo continues recollecting his glory days, oblivious to the escalating passion. He suddenly realizes his tales regarding his wild days as a womanizing cowboy may not bolster his mystery-solving narrative. Stopping himself mid-sentence, he finishes the story with a different selection of words. "... ghosts in my time."

The comments are of no consequence. It is as though he does not exist in the coach's small cabin. The couple's infatuation persists, and after being kicked several times by flailing feet, he decides it is best to exit. "Well, you two lovebirds, it has been a pleasure. I am tuckered out from fighting like cats, so I'm just going to let y'all have your privacy. *Adios*, get on to it," he says.

Grabbing the knob, he twists the metal, opening the door to leave. Sid hears the clicking noise signaling his departure and pulls away from Jubilee to address Alonzo. "One last thing, Bronc Buster."

Alonzo turns to listen to what he has to say. "Yeah, Boss Man?"

The Sheriff smirks and taps the shiny badge on his shirt. "Now, don't you get too boozy tonight celebrating. I'm a man of my word, so that bargain we made starts tomorrow."

The men share a smile and nod, and Alonzo exits the carriage into the crisp darkness with a final tip of his hat.

I have to say, the stars looked mighty beautiful that night, almost like small silver coins twinkling in the sky.

Six

ℋaunted 𝒲ine 𝒞ellar

1864, Wild West Saloon

I hope y'all have enjoyed the story, because we are back with the off-kilter Preacher man and the chucklehead bar.

Alonzo Bill smirks back in the Shooting Iron Saloon, still reminiscing about the memory. *I reckon everyone knows of how I bedded that ghost down.* He proudly adjusts the bolo tie around his neck and polishes the silver tips to a sparkle. Trying to knock the other man out of his stooped-over slump, he chuckles and hits his back to instigate a compliment.

Hunched over in his seat, the blow to his back causes the Preacher's reflexes to kick in, and his posture straightens. He refrains from looking at the cowboy and nods while gathering his bearings. "The

Sheriff said you are the best demon fighter there ever was," he says.

As the ranch hand listens to the compliment, he closes his eyes and takes a deep breath to allow each word to soak into his ears. Opening his eyelids, he drops his hands to brush a piece of lint off his jacket and stares at the bottles of alcohol on the shelf behind the bar. The light flickering from the candles reflects colored speckles from the bottles into the white irises of his gleaming eyes. "Ain't that the truth. Did he tell you about the ghostly cellar?" he asks.

Feeling a memory come back of the moment, he pays no attention to Preacher Boone nodding. "I reckon so," the Preacher says.

If only he knew the actual story, he may or may not have hired my skin for this job. There are no other cowboys in this line of work, so he probably still would have hired me for whatever his spooky predicament. Oh, what the Hell? Since nothing is happening on the daughter front at the Saloon, we have adequate time for another story of my glorious accounts in this town.

Rather than get into a scuffle, let's leave his conniption-filled ass for a minute so that I can learn you a proper understanding of the ghostly cellar. Grab your lassos, because we are about to ride back in time. Also, don't forget to put on a full leather get-up, because that cellar was colder than a witch's tit.

1861, Whitley Cellar

Darkness falls upon the cold winter's eve. Frigid air rolls through the desert terrain, kicking up dirt with sporadic gusts. A dark brown house sits a lengthy distance from the town's main road, perched behind a handcrafted picket fence of chestnut tones. Several feet from the house sit two shutter doors flush against a mounded patch of dry grass.

The clamoring slatted wood calls two men trekking from the house's front doors. Tilting the brim of his hat to cover his face, Alonzo follows behind a small man wearing a buttoned vest and bow tie. His trousers are deep black and blend into the darkness. His sleeves are crafted of pinstripe black-and-white fabric variations and rolled to his elbows. Upon his chipmunk face sits a well-curled handlebar mustache with days' worth of hardened wax, and small wireframe reading glasses are perched on the bridge of his nose.

Carrying a candle-fueled lantern, he leads the way across the unevenly packed dirt and purses his lips to concentrate. He is unfazed by the outside elements. The cowboy does not reciprocate with the same easy-going personality. His leather overcoat is buttoned from top to bottom. He pulls each lapel towards one another to help warm his neck and shield his skin from the bite of the relentless wind. Following close in step, he shuffles his feet and looks to the ground so dust does not infiltrate his corneas. As a mighty gust of dirt-ridden air pelts the left side of his body, he opens his mouth to speak and inhales a mouthful of dry grime textured like sand. His lips blow puffs of air to spit the unwanted intruders off his tongue. "Jiminy, Doc, you make all that money. Couldn't you have moved that wine cellar closer to your sleeping quarters?" he asks.

Each turbulent gust of wind sends the unlatched shutters flapping and screeching as the two men stop in front of the commotion. Passing the lamp to the cowman, the small-statured man takes a deep breath as he leads the way, ignoring the ranch hand's chatter. He bends down to open the cellar doors, and with a great heave, the wooden shutters catch a gust of wind and swing open wildly.

Silently, the small man reaches behind him for the lamp and leads their way down a rickety set of porous wood steps. Following close behind, Alonzo shrugs off the lack of conversation and scans the room to grasp the nature of the task. His spur catches on a splintered step leading to the bottom of the room, and he stumbles. Without missing a beat, his hand clutches onto the railing as his spurs continue to clink down the remaining steps until reaching the basement's stone floor.

Alonzo stands up from his sprawled position, brushes off his pants, and reroutes his dampened ego. Shifting his gaze, he eyes the man as he pulls the candle from the confines of the lantern. Moving through the room with a sense of familiarity, he lights several candelabras throughout the dingy cellar. Each flickering wick highlights the bottles of booze lining the surrounding walls, causing Alonzo's eyes to grow wide with excitement.

He spots one bottle's familiarity and rushes over to admire the label. "Oh, Doggies, do I have memories with this whiskey right here." He picks up the container and analyzes it as wild memories from the booze-filled, women-laden night replay in his mind. "I bet many boot-lickers have tried to swindle this gem from you." The bottle makes his throat dry with thirst.

The older man ignores his admiration as he finishes lighting the last candle and puts the original one back in the lantern for safety. He clears his throat to get the cowboy back on track and uses the dim lantern to light the mounted shelves. "As I was saying, something has been knocking firewater off this rack, and I fear it's spooky in nature," he says.

Alonzo takes one last lustful glimpse at the bottle in his hand and gently places it back on the rack. Turning away from his vice, he locks eyes on the shaken man, and with his eyebrows rounding his look of concern, he speaks. "Spooks, huh?"

The man gulps, squeezing his hand tighter around the lantern's handle to stop his trembling limbs. "I'm telling you, I know this may sound a little crazy--" he says as his hand lifts to help diffuse judgment.

Before he can finish his plea for understanding, the cowboy cracks his knuckles and approaches him. "No need for all that. Remember, you're talking to a bona fide ghostbuster, so nothing seems cracked," he says with a lighthearted chuckle.

Feeling comfortable expressing his speculations without fear of judgment, the nervous man lets out a deep sigh of relief. His demeanor relaxes, and his mouth moves at the speed of light, spewing wild accusations. "My ex-rib's Momma is haunting me from her rotten dirt-filled grave. Please don't ask me how, but I just know it." Afraid his harsh words may have upset the ghost; he peers around the room and covers his mouth with his hands to stop himself from continuing.

The outburst leaves the cowboy in shock, and he stares at the grown man while trying to fight back his building internal laughter. "Well, I have to hand it to you, Doc, this is a first," he says. Taking a fast glance away to gain his composure, he places his fingers against his forehead to recenter his thoughts. "I got to ask you something personal before we start."

Wanting nothing more than freedom from being haunted by the angry spirit, the man nods his head in compliance. Taking a deep inhale, Alonzo turns to face him. "What did you do to make the old hen mad as a March hare?" he asks.

As he takes a moment, Alonzo reads the expression across the small man's face and realizes it has struck a nerve. He waves his hand in a sweeping motion to cancel out his inquisition. "Never mind. The reason for your haunting doesn't matter. It's as right as rain, Doc."

Worried his probing may jeopardize his paycheck, he changes course and begins walking around the room to inspect for clues of haunting. All of Doc's irritation subsides as his focus shifts to biting his nails and anticipating the worst. As he studies the hired expert inspecting the room's floor, he follows behind, waiting with bated breath for any observation that validates his fear.

Along his second sweep of the room walls, Alonzo spots a hole that a burrowing rat has made. Thinking swiftly on his feet, he stops in front of it and motions for the man to shine the lantern towards the discovery. "Come close; I reckon I see a spirit hole," he says as he gets down on all fours to get a better view.

As Doc holds his lantern, he scratches his head to ponder. "Um... 'spirit hole?'" he asks with hesitation.

Playing off his gullible naivety, Alonzo's lips spew a chuckle at the question, and he turns his head to address Doc in his confused state. "I'm acock that a man like yourself doesn't know what a spirit hole is." After a moment of pause, he motions for him to hand him the lantern, so he can better light the mysterious cave. "You better feel lucky you hired an expert, because lemme tell you, Doc, this isn't looking peachy. This here is a portal to the blazes dug deep. I reckon the best comparison I got is it's like a beehive for ghosts," he says.

The poor man stationed behind him scoots closer and hides, peering from behind the opening in the wall. His knees quiver with terror and his teeth chatter with building nervousness. "So, they all are hiding there?" he asks as his shaking hand points. "With that horrible woman?"

Standing frozen in place, intently staring at the hole, he refrains from shifting his gaze and answers with a nod. "Now, this isn't a battle for the faint of heart, Doc." Lowering his voice to the quietest of tones, he turns slightly toward the hovering man and whispers, "They can smell human fear."

The single statement causes the older man's eyes to bulge in terror and his mouth to fall open into a gaping look of shock. The cowboy feeds into his spiraling imagination and seizes the opportunity to play up the drama-filled escapade. Snapping his head back toward the harmless hole, his tongue makes clicking sounds behind the back molars of his teeth. Each of the high-pitched *ticks* echoes between the dingy walls.

Alonzo, exhibiting textbook fear, turns to make eye contact with Doc. "You hear that?" he asks.

Common sense eludes the man due to his heightened anxiety, and the sound causes his pupils to dilate with fear. His foot no longer contains its composure, but begins wildly tapping, and his jittery squirming follows suit. He's jumping at every sound, real or imagined, and his terrified eyes dart around the room as they try to pinpoint the cause of each noise. "As clear as Easter Day!" he says.

Alonzo Bill stands with the lantern, brushes the dirt from his knees, and shakes his head. To calm his high-strung bones, Doc hands the flickering searchlight to the customer for safekeeping. Placing his hands on the man's shoulders, Alonzo stares him in the center of each iris. "Sometimes these spirits become awful angry when I tell them to git. If I were you, I would stay clear of my wrangling and wait right up those stairs 'til it's safe. I want none of my customers to get hurt; it would tarnish my reputation. After shoving the ghost back into its hidey-hole, I will sound a whistle that the coast is clear for you to come back."

Doc listens intently to every word and, with a large gulp, stops his chitter-chattering teeth and wags his head to show agreement. "I reckon that's a good idea," he says. Clutching onto the handle of the light source tighter, he flees up the staircase, his feet carrying him at the speed of a prize-winning racehorse. The only sound louder than frenzied stomping up the stairs is the cellar doors slamming shut behind him.

Left alone in the dingy cellar, Alonzo raises his palm to his right ear, listening for the locking latch. As soon as it falls into place with a *clack*, his theatrical posture subsides, and his body spins in a slow circle as he scans the room to verify that he is alone. Each candle reflects off the row of alcohol bottles, colorful glass lighting every direction with a multicolored prism show. The spectacular view causes his eyes to widen with excitement. A gnawing sensation stems from the pit of his stomach, alerting his tongue to lick his lips to quench their parched state.

Closing his eyes, he imagines the soothing taste of the alcohol lining the shelves in front of him. As they reopen, they are pleasantly met with the view of the well-aged whiskey he had pointed out earlier. Unable to control his desires, he walks towards the luring container, grasps it, and chuckles as he caresses it with his hands. Without battling his whim, he uses his silver-studded belt buckle, which features a bucking bronco, to help open the bottle, then happily chugs the contents.

He lowers the bottle from his thirsty lips to assess the damage done. Realizing the situation may appear suspicious if the man were to return to find only his bottle of sought-after whiskey half-emptied, he sees no choice but to put on a show for the eavesdropper waiting on the other side of the cellar door.

Getting into character, he runs around the room, howling to simulate the sounds of a fighting ghost. He gets out of breath while wrestling with himself, which proves advantageous, as it causes him to huff and puff, adding an element of authenticity to the event. "I will not tell you again, ghost, you got to leave that Doc alone!" he shouts.

Chugging the remaining contents of the open container, he chucks the empty bottle against the floor. The enormous crash of glass creates a loud shattering noise that echoes through the damp space and up the staircase. The alcohol begins to take effect. His words slur as he yells into the air, "I repent you from this here cellar, demon!" Continuing his loud ruckus, he staggers to the shelf, picking up more bottles to sample and break.

Amongst the shards of glass strewn across the floor, he observes a tiny mouse watching his charade from the rodent hole in the room's corner. Disgusted by the filthy creature, he gets down on all fours and shoos the mouse back into the hole's depths. Upon its retreat, he grabs the smallest remaining bottle from the shelf and forcefully wedges it into the opening. "I mean it! Cut and run, ghost! Cut and run!" he yells.

Allowing himself a moment to catch his breath, he stands to look at the damage done and brushes his hands together to rid them of grime. Pleased with his accomplishment, his lips blare a whistle. "Coast is clear, Doc!"

The cellar door slowly opens with a loud creak, and the harsh sound causes the flashback to dissipate.

That was that. All I had to do was rid the man of the varmint responsible for breaking his booze.

1864, Wild West Saloon

The Preacher adjusts the stool underneath him, and it screeches against the wood, mimicking the creaking wine cellar doors. Alonzo Bill snaps to attention, his eyes shifting from the magnificent line of alluring handcrafted bottles behind the bar to the obnoxious chair. As preacher Boone reflects on Doc's version of the story, he replies. "Sure did. Doc said you cleaned that ghost's plow real good."

I reckon this is the first bar I've ever gotten tired of seeing, Alonzo thinks as he realizes he is still in the Shooting Iron Saloon.

Seven

The Witchy Nipper

Alonzo Bill puffs out his chest proudly, thinking of how he pulled the wool over the town's eyes, and smirks. "What about the Witchy nipper?" he asks.

Hearing the name out loud causes Preacher Boone to shutter.

Don't worry your little heads while we wait for the little lady's grand arrival. I'll fill you in on the inside details of the account, and this one is even more bonkers than the last. Poor Elizabeth Townshed... but I can't say I wasn't happy with that easy money train entering the station.

Before I get too carried away, I'll tell you the real story of what happened, and you will be happy to know it's a short one.

1862, Townshed Family Home

The early afternoon falls over the perfectly kempt home's exterior. Every sunbeam ray shoots brightly through the clouds and illuminates the red paint on each shingle of the newly touched-up barn. A row of neatly laid oxidized brick leads to the front door.

Alonzo Bill houses a wad of chew inside his bottom lip and takes a moment to inhale the rose-filled air. His ratty wardrobe has progressed from the other two missions. He is stylized in all-black leather, and the suede texture is ideally brushed in the same direction. Before starting his bold entrance into the house, he spits his wad of chew onto the immaculate lawn. The darkened cluster barely misses the pristinely laid bricks beneath his feet.

As he picks up each boot to walk, his lips smile at his polished spurs clicking against the hard surface. He exudes confidence, as he has more experience under his belt, and his upgraded belt buckle adds to his feeling of invincibility. The farmland scenery reminds him of his childhood, and he slows the pace of his steps to cherish the nostalgic smells of dewy alfalfa and pine trees.

A woman frantically peers out the picture window facing the front yard, and her hazel eyes look relieved at the sight of the cowboy. She frantically leaves the picturesque view and opens the door to greet his slowpoke pace.

The door's ungreased hinges announce her entrance with a shrill, and the sound catches the cowman's attention. Quickly, he focuses away from a swaying pine tree's calming presence to make the younger woman's acquaintance. Her appeal is abrasive, and jars his mind from its euphoric daze. As she frantically flags him down with her bony arms, his observing eyes stare at the puffed dark circles under her eyes and the flannel nightgown hanging on her body. Her hair is tied up in makeshift rag curlers made from frayed pieces of an old bed sheet.

Stomping her feet to urge him to hurry kicks up a light sheet of dust from the wooden plank porch and dirties her toes. "Hey there, I'm Elizabeth Townshed! I reckon you must be the cowboy my husband hired to help. You are even taller and more handsome than I expected."

He tips the brim of his new black cowboy hat to acknowledge her accurate assessment and smirks. "I reckon you are correct," he says as he walks up the steps of the house.

An awkward smile forms on her face, but swiftly dissipates. As she watches him take the last step up the porch, she turns to hurry inside the home, motioning for him to follow.

Even though her short-lived flirtation is unusual for him, he brushes off his ego and, with a shrug of his shoulders, follows her inside. As soon as the door shuts behind him, the sound of a screaming infant pierces his eardrums. Lifting his hands to cover his ear holes, he tries to hide his annoyance and changes the subject, commenting on the chaotic state of the house. "You got a wild animal living in here?"

Being overtired, the comment doesn't faze her, and without stopping, she starts walking up the wooden staircase. "This way now," she says over her shoulder.

Alonzo follows close behind, and as the sound becomes louder, his face dramatically scrunches. To fix the situation quickly and end the obnoxious sound, he increases his pace to match hers.

As soon as they reach the top step, she ushers him into a nearby room directly in front of them. Once they are inside, she shuts the door to quiet the noise and races to the crib, picking up the crying newborn to coddle. She carries the screaming babe to a hand-carved rocking chair stationed in the room's corner and neurotically begins rocking back and forth to soothe it. The hushing sounds cause the baby's face to grow a darker shade of red, and she panics.

Alonzo refrains from exposing his true feelings for the screaming baby and walks across the room to show sympathy. "I bet you're fit to be tied, dealing with the ruckus of a witchy babe," he says.

She tries to fight back the tears from her sleep-deprived eyes as she moves the chair faster. "I'm telling you, it ain't normal. That baby girl has been fussing day and night without stopping," she says.

Leaving one toe stationary on the pine planks, she continues to rock the child while she lifts the other foot to point at a nearby Bible stained with vomit on the other side of the room. "I even looked at the words of sweet baby Jesus's bible over there, and all I know for certain is, this child must be a witch."

She stares at the approaching cowboy with a look of despair, and her bloodshot eyes cry for help. "I fear you are the only hope my poor babe has left. I don't know what else I can do."

Looking at the wailing child's face, he fixates on its flush gums and gurgling screams. Reluctantly, he sticks out his arms to take the load. "All right then, lemme see it."

Without pausing, she hops from the rocker and all but throws the baby in his arms. Her eyes intently watch his next moves.

Finding it increasingly difficult to hide his disdain, he holds the infant an arm's distance away. "Leave us be, and I will rid this child of the witchy nature."

As he glances up to obtain her approval, the bedroom door slams, and she is gone. Immediately, he yells after her, "I'll whistle at you when it's safe to come back in."

Knowing they are alone, he lets down the mask covering his annoyance and stares into the crying baby's welting eyes. "Well, aren't you a sight," he chuckles.

The baby's howl grows louder. With each scream, it starts to hyperventilate more, becoming lost in hysterics. Drool drips from the corners of its mouth, its stomach contracts to catch each breath, and a grotesque combination of noises sound in its diaper.

Fighting his disgust, he reluctantly places the baby on his shoulder and pats its back. With a loud, aggressive belch, the small child falls silent. Alonzo catches a glimpse of the baby's eyes closing.

As the child drifts off to sleep, both tiny nostrils release vibrating snores, and the cowboy loudly whistles for its mother. "You're safe to come back now! The nipper is rid of the witch!" he shouts.

The sound of the door opening marks the end of his reminiscing.

1864, Wild West Saloon

As his eyes open, he notices his arms still mimicking holding the child from the daydream, and his entire body shudders at the thought of a screaming baby. The mere retelling of the tale agitates him. Looking around to appreciate the scenario, he is relieved to find himself back in the daunting structure of the Shooting Iron Saloon.

Just imagining the possessed child makes Preacher Boone tremble with fear. "That was a scare," he says.

If only he knew the half of it. I made a slab of cash from that transaction. Honestly, some of my biggest and best-paying clients have been new parents. They are always so nerve-driven with their actions and unaware of the ways children fuss. I mean, he's a parent, isn't he?

Anyway, before I nod off, that's enough of that. Let's jump to a story I know the Preacher will be asking about. This one, holds a special place in my heart. It's the tale of the Skookum horse. Yippee Ki-Yay, let us keep this cattle roundup going.

Eight

The Skookum Horse

1863, Buck Farm

Small glimpses of the rising sun peek through clusters of distant cacti scattered across the sweeping terrain of the desert. A small barn made of mismatched logs sits on an obscure patch of thirsty farmland that breaks up the desolate monotony, and its colorless exterior matches the muted dirt floor. Six horse stalls line the inside wall of the falling structure, surrounded by broken fence pieces.

To any sound-minded person, it would have been obvious the man was cheap, but he told everyone the same story: He refrained from giving any of the walls a permanent stain to preserve the wood's natural appearance. Maybe that's why we got along so well; he was a great storyteller, like me.

Anyhow, let's get back to it.

George Buck, a farmer who looks to be in his early thirties, leads the observant buckaroo through the rustic barn doors. His calloused hands, dirt-packed fingernails, and work clothes decorated with stains display proof of years of outdoor manual labor. Halfway inside, a loose board on the bottom of the door frame catches the side of his clunky oversized work boot, almost pulling it off his foot. His arms flail as he regains his balance, and with strawberry-red cheeks, he points his quivering finger at the culprit that caused his embarrassment. "Go to Jericho, you lousy piece of wood," he says as he angrily kicks the wood back into place to teach it a lesson.

A gust of wind picks up dust and disperses it through the air. Ignoring the man's rant, Alonzo quickly steps around the off-kilter board to escape the grit blowing into his eyes.

The door shutting behind him provokes a single distressed whinny that continues to bounce around the open room. As the sound enters Alonzo Bill's ears, the aroma of hay and earthy grain wafts into his nostrils. It reminds him of his labor-intensive days working on a farmstead, and the warmth from the nostalgia places a smile on his face. His eyes follow the noise to identify the culprit, landing on the horse stall furthest from the door.

The anxious mustang continues to neigh and buck wildly in its wooden confinement at the end of the row. Its lush white coat is sweaty, and foam coats its neck and chest. As the spooked creature's nerves escalate, its front hooves strike at the walls that cage it. The repetitive collision creates vibrations that resonate through the wood, knocking a bridle and reins off a hanger fashioned from a repurposed rusted horseshoe.

Alonzo feels the room come to a halt. Pulled to the distressed steed like a mother to a crying child, he moves closer until he stands directly before the stallion's stall. "Whoa, there. You are a mighty beautiful creature, aren't you?" he says, raising his hand to calm the magnificent beast. The horse rears, striking its hooves at the door. Alonzo raises his hands higher and chuckles. "I know. I would be as mad as a wet cat if they confined me in a wooden cell. I reckon everything's going to be okay."

Still bothered by the embarrassment of his clumsy entrance, the farmhand remains stationed near the barn entrance, pouting. He picks up a dried alfalfa stock that escaped a hay bale, pops one end in his mouth, and chews on the green fiber. His back straightens, and he crosses his arms, sarcastically laughing in a judging tone at the retired cowboy's horse-taming strategy.

A lack of acknowledgment from Alonzo causes frustration to brew inside his gut. Wanting to add his two cents, he lifts his finger to gain attention like a kid in a one-room schoolhouse. "That there is the most wicked horse I've ever seen. I tried climbing aboard that stallion yesterday and damn near broke my back in two. As you can see, it's still wearing its saddle. I couldn't get near it again to take the dadgum thing off. I had to chase the beast back into its stall, bucking and rearing all the way. Just lucky I could get the door closed. "

Hoping to engage, but still ignored, he raises his voice even louder to be heard. "Want to know what I think?"

Alonzo, annoyed by the farmhand's babbling interjections, ignores him and takes a step closer to the stall, continuing to keep his focus solely on the horse.

With more to say and insistent on being heard, the farmhand yells to the end of the barn. "Plain as day, that there stallion is off its nuts, by golly. The devil itself has taken over that horse's mind."

Raising his hand to his face, he points to his pupils and continues his rant. "You see them blackened eyes. The way it stares isn't usual. If that isn't the mark of hell, I tell you what, you can call me a liar and tie me to a pew." He stands still for a moment after his lengthy sermon. Huffing and puffing like a freight train, he bends over to catch his breath.

Alonzo turns his head just enough that the ranting farmer cannot see him roll his eyes and mouth the words "Dumb ass." Clearing his throat, he puts on a straight face and turns back toward the ruffled man. "I reckon I can rid the creature of the devil's blood," he says.

The farmer's breathing calms, and the barn falls silent. Scratching his head in disbelief that a cure is possible, but having no other options, he shrugs with a lengthy sigh. "I reckon you are the expert on the topic, so, by all means, you are the best option we got," he says as he spins around to exit.

Alonzo is relieved to watch the man leave, and the absence of his annoying presence allows his posture to relax and slouch. Just as he thinks he is free of the menace, the man stops and turns around to add one last word. He throws both hands in the air. "Shoot, you don't have to tell me twice. I'm as gone as thieves," he says.

The retired cowboy nods to get rid of him and waits for him to finish his exit. As the door shuts, he shakes his head and moves closer to the stallion's stall. Extending a hand through the cutout in the door, he attempts to touch its nose. "How'd you end up hulled up with a yack like him?" he says.

The white mustang throws his head and rears to escape Alonzo's touch, and a loud whinny blares from his open mouth and flared nostrils.

Knowing he must change his approach, Alonzo retracts his hand. Slowly, he unlatches the door and opens it, confident that becoming well-acquainted with the distressed creature will calm its agitation. He stretches his hand toward the steed to build trust, allowing it to become familiar with his smell. After only two giant sniffs, the stallion stands still, and Alonzo steps inside. "I don't blame you for wrinkling your spine," he says.

As he lightly strokes the horse's neck, the fingers of his opposite hand slide underneath the cinch of the saddle and encounter a cactus burr. "If I wore something constricting and prickly, I would be mad as a hornet, too." Sensing the animal settle, he chuckles, loosens the leather cinch strap, and removes the thorny debris.

Immediate relief overtakes the stallion, and he nuzzles Alonzo with his nose to show thanks. He places his hand on the top of the horse's head, cherishing their deep connection. "I'd take you with me if I could," he says. Emotions well in his chest, and he clears his throat to suppress their escape.

Gaining his composure, he places two fingers in the corners of his mouth between his lips and sounds a loud whistle. "All right, sodbuster, you can come back in now. I rid the creature of all that is Sam Hill!"

His voice cracks through his summoning shout, and he wiggles his nose to deter a welling tear.

1864, Wild West Saloon

As his mind returns to the bar, he rotates his shoulder to mask his emotions and sniffles as he ruminates over the special bond created with the white stallion,

For those of you concerned with what happened to him when I left, don't be. After collecting payment for services, I returned to the barn in the dead of night and set the sucker free. He remains my faithful companion to this day.

The story of the stallion brings a coy grin to his lips.

The Preacher, looking for reassurance, pulls his hands away from his face and turns toward the cowboy. "The sheriff said you did an expelling of spirits on a farmer's mustang," he says.

As Alonzo turns to answer the despairing man, he sees that all the melted candles forming the pentagram flames have turned black, and for a brief second, the oddity sets him back.

Shaking his shoulders to rid himself of the heebie-jeebies, he disallows any doubts from entering his head and focuses only on his past accomplishments. Turning to face the hopeful man sitting next to him, he chuckles and tips his hat. "Sure did. I knocked the skookum right out of him."

The reassuring words bring the Preacher a bit of security, and he stutters with newfound clarity. "I reckon that's why the Sheriff told me you'd be perfect for helping my sweet little Ophelia."

Alonzo stands taller and polishes the silver bolo tie around his neck while absorbing every word falling from the preacher's lips. He relishes in the ego-stroking compliments. "Well, considering I'm the best there is, I'd say the Sheriff is correct with his judgment."

Basking in his glory, his fingers reach in the leather pouch slung around his hips, and he pulls out the makings for a cigarette. With the stick rolled and resting in his mouth, he lowers himself to the floor and lights it on the nearest candle's black flame. Upon standing, he jokingly nudges the Preacher's shoulder while blowing a ring in the air. "So now, Converter, where is this '*sweet little Ophelia*?'"

After a moment and no response to his question, Alonzo looks over at his compadre.

Preacher Boone's demeanor has drastically shifted. He stares blankly into the distant darkness, mouth gaping open, unresponsive, with horror plastered over his face. His tongue uselessly jostles in his mouth, trying to form words, but only an airy stutter emerges.

The muted response amuses the cowboy. He takes a long inhalation of his cigarette and moves closer to the trembling man to gain his attention, adjusting his body to a partial squat to match eye levels. As he assesses the man's catatonic state, his eyes drift to his shaking knees, and he busts out in laughter, almost dropping the burning cigarette. "You, Preacher, are in worse shape than a cat in a roomful of rockers. I think you're the one who needs this relaxing stick hanging from my lips."

The lack of response annoys Alonzo, and he tries to engage the Preacher by playfully slapping his shoulder, but the man continues staring into the room's dark abyss. Without a word spoken, he slowly lifts his jittery hand and points towards the top of the stairs.

The room's temperature drops below freezing, and something doesn't settle right with the cowboy. He slowly turns to look in the direction the petrified finger is pointing.

Nine

You Must Be Ophelia

1864, Wild West Saloon

A dark wooden staircase protrudes from the far corner across the room. The last step mounted to the bottom floorboards has a slight dip and resembles the basin of a dried-up waterfall. Each tread leading to the second floor is narrower than the one before, and a railing crafted from yellowing antlers guides the journey to the top.

The buckaroo's forehead furrows as he squints to get a better look--his left hand rests on his hip, and his right acts as an awning across his eyebrow. Slowly, both pupils adjust to the darkness and scan the stairway to the shadowed top in hopes of glimpsing what's terrifying the man beside him.

He makes out a frail framed figure standing on the top step and pauses as a series of light, raspy breaths reverberate through the bar. "Well, I'll be damned," he says with an exhalation of relief.

A peculiarly positioned eleven-year-old girl wearing a dirty nightgown hunches over her locked legs. Her jarring position showcases the waist-long length of her scraggly ash-brown hair, and its dark color contrasts against her ghostly pale skin. Bruises from long-term use of leather restraints cover both wrists, and her nails are blackened with an unhealthy blue hue. The flickering flames at the bottom of the stairs light her facial features, accenting the crust on her lips. Her unkempt nightgown shares the same off-putting greenish yellow stain on Preacher Boone's lapel.

Alonzo lowers his cupped right hand from his brow to his chin. "Huh," he says. He closely takes stock of her hamstrung movement and unnatural stance and thinks about how uncomfortable each vertebra must be in carrying out the gestures. A brief reflection convinces him she must have scoliosis. With sarcasm, he places his hand upon his back as he stoops over, simulating her intolerable posture, and turns to the Preacher to clarify that he is on their scam. "If it isn't the small fry herself," he says as he chuckles. He slaps the man's paralyzed shoulder and grins, then turns back to face the child at the top of the stairs.

With a nerve-fueled gulp, the Preacher's Adam's apple slowly moves from his jawline to his clavicle.

The cowboy takes a few steps closer to the stairs, his gaze fixated on the despondent child. He stomps his feet, rattling his spurs against the floor to break her stare and gain her attention. Seeing no response, he's irritated by the disrespect shown by the girl. He releases a passive chuckle and clears his throat to mask his frustration. With the cigarette still hanging from his lips, he lifts his hands to form a funnel around his mouth, so he can project his voice louder. "You must be the loco filly I'm here to visit."

The preacher remains seated at the bar, still frozen in a trance. The harsh inflection behind the mystery solver's words makes him fearful of how his child may respond. His eyes widen to focus on her movements, and he desperately wants to warn the fool of the potential risks of taunting her.

Through the silence, Alonzo catches the Preacher starting to speak in the grip of the moment, and quickly raises his hand to quiet him. In a show of dominance, he puffs out his chest to stand taller and, without turning around, directs his speech at his anxious employer. Tiny bits of ash fall to the floor from his smoke as his lips rustle to speak. "You know, Converter, I appreciate the effort y'all put into this dog-and-pony show, but come on now. We both know that girl up there is just looking a little bushed, and that's that," he says. His head swivels to assess his response.

Instead of giving a rebuttal, the Preacher's pupils grow dilated, and his molars chatter.

Feeling he is getting nowhere in his attempt to glean information, and fed up with their amateur performances, Alonzo turns back toward the child. As his irises point toward the girl's crooked back, he catches the slightest movement, and boisterously claps his hands together. While emulating stagnant applause, his face turns a shade of pink. Weary from the combination of the late hour and an excess of booze, he can no longer hide his impatience.

Gradually, the child's long, matted hair parts at her forehead as her head lifts to acknowledge the noise abrasively coming from below. Each jarring movement reveals new facial features, starting with her darkened vascular eyes and condescending purple smirk. She takes her time to revel in the mockery and adjusts every unnaturally shaped joint that causes the off-kilter placement of her feet. Her grimy bare feet move toward one another to fix her unaligned hips. As her disjointed hips move into place, the loudly snapping bone echoes down the steps, and her smirk deepens.

Every slow movement feels like ridicule and feeds the agitation nestled in his core. Continuing to let the rest of the smoking stick burn between his lips, he claps his hands like a thunderstorm and loudly snaps his fingers to get her attention. "Lil' Ophelia, I reckon you best be coming down here now," he says, pointing to the floor by his boots.

He finds the lack of her willingness to listen to his commands frustrating and her bratty attitude unacceptable. He neurotically inhales a few large puffs of nicotine as his boot taps. "Girl, I'm about to become awful sore about this here exchange between us if you don't come on down on the count of three."

She methodically moves her fingers with a stone-cold smile plastered on her face. One by one, each of her small knuckles unleashes a cracking explosion.

Alonzo loudly grunts to show the extent of his frustration, and his pupils shoot dagger-filled glances at the unresponsive, useless father glued to the bar stool behind him. Alonzo blames her misbehaving tendencies on the man's poor parenting and reckons he owes him a helping hand in getting her to listen.

Seeing no other option, he takes matters into his own hands. As he shifts his weight to face the disobedient girl, his fists tightly clenched, he says, "All right, I am about to start a-countin', and you better get your spindly ass down here by the time I get to three."

With the sinister grin still across her lips, her neck stretches, allowing her head to rotate abnormally in a circular motion. As the back of her skull grazes her shoulder blades, the front of her chest protrudes and spasms.

A look of disgust falls over Alonzo's face, as he finds the weird mannerism of the child off-putting. Every cracking bone and contortion causes his mouth to gape open and his words to take a pause. Basking in the repulsiveness of her presentation, he turns his attention to the father. Before he can speak, both lids of his eyes wince like eating a sour lemon, and his hand raises to catch the man's attention. Not finding success in his attempt, he walks closer, reaches for the bar stool beside the Preacher, noisily drags it out from under the bar top, and sits down to meet his eye level.

The sound's shrill piercing of the cold air causes the Preacher's preserved state to evaporate. His body flinches as both his peepers move to the cowboy.

"Now I got to acknowledge the corn with you, man to man," Alonzo says. Thinking of the girl's blatant disrespect causes agitated jitters to roll through his bones, and his speech escalates louder. "Before I came in this here saloon, I was fair to the middling. If she doesn't stop this nonsense and get a wiggle on soon, I swear, I am gonna get mighty riled up." Alonzo attempts to take another hit off his cigarette, and, realizing it has burned down to the butt, he smashes it into the top of the wooden bar stool.

The Preacher's focus fixates on the oddly satisfying motion of Alonzo's squashing fingers. As he perceives the cowhand's aggrandized and cocky personality has curtailed to something a bit more relatable, he relaxes his stiff nature.

Watching a small heap of ash continue to build beneath the demolished butt causes Alonzo to reminisce about how the girl's matted ash-colored locks parted, exposing her mocking grin. His hand abruptly shoots into the sky, and he holds up a single finger to begin the countdown. "One!" he shouts.

The Preacher's hands scramble, frantically waving toward Alonzo, desperately trying to silence him. "I reckon I would cut that off before she gets madder than a hornet," he says.

His threatening tone is surprising, and Alonzo finds the dramatic nature of his panicked state an entertaining twist to the evening's events. No longer able to maintain a straight face over the ridiculous theatrics, he laughs. "Preacher, that child just needs a good whooping."

The men lose touch with their surroundings, distracted by their idle banter, while Ophelia silently stirs. Her arms bend at her elbows, forming a reversed ninety-degree angle. As they rise to the height of her shoulders, her contorted frame resembles a scarecrow swaying in an abandoned corn field.

Stubbornly refusing to break eye contact, Alonzo's smirk widens across his face. "Two..." he says. He springs up from his seat and paces the bar with an obnoxious chuckle, stopping only to give her the what for.

Spinning on his heels, he glances at the Preacher, who has burrowed his head into his hands, hoping it will all go away. After finding him useless, he turns back toward Ophelia. "I was hoping it wouldn't come to this but, its look-in like your gonna force my tongue to count to three, aren't you, Ophelia?"

Filled with disbelief, he shakes his head angrily from side to side with frustration as he resumes his pacing and dramatic display. "You know, little girl, I'm getting mighty ticked."

The discolored whites of Ophelia's irises consume her eyes, and her colorless stare riddles the cowboy.

Noticing that no one is listening, Alonzo throws up his hands. "I already had to put up hearing your pappy yarn on for hours," he says as he points to the coward at the bar.

Receiving no validation, he continues his rant, and glimpsing the shelves of alcohol from the corner of his eye further instigates his tirade, reminding him of the poor service he received. "Don't even get me going about that bar dog they keep in here. Oh, boy. Oh, boy!" he says.

Even though no one responds, venting lifts a weight from his shoulders, and the action causes him to laugh hysterically. "Since that bar dog is long gone, and this little performance has been going on longer than it should, I say it's time for an intermission. You just hold your horses, and I will get back to you in two ticks of a pocket watch."

Everyone remains still in their position, and he takes the lack of interjection as consent for his behavior. "I'm going to fetch me a drink so, you can wait right up there, Ophelia. Just keep on doing what you're doing."

Shrugging, he briefly removes his black cowboy hat, runs his fingers through his hair, pushes his sun-kissed locks from his face, and securely positions his hat back on his head. The sight of the alcohol bottles causes a hankering thirst to take over his throat. Taking a running start, he slides over the top of the bar.

The sound of Alonzo's silver belt buckle scraping against the bar's freshly polished wood makes the Preacher jump in his seat. Looking at his daughter and seeing she has yet to move, he shifts his attention to the out-of-control cowhand. "What in God's name are you doing, Bushwhacker?" he asks.

Alonzo lands on the server-side of the counter and pays no attention to anyone as he reaches for an aged bottle of whiskey on the top shelf.

Without waiting for an answer, the Preacher leaps to his feet to stop the hired hand from drinking more booze. His efforts fall short, and he helplessly sees the cowboy pop the bottle's cork and chug its contents.

As Alonzo gets a load of the frantic man running toward him, he guzzles faster. Finishing half of the container, he lowers the bottle from his face and wipes the residue from his lips, then releases a muted belch.

Heavily panting, the frazzled Preacher rounds the corner of the bar out of breath from his short sprint.

Alonzo signals him to stop, as he attempts to act sober, his words slur, and his stance waivers. "I reckon, Converter, I'm just trying to make hay while the sun still shines," he says with a hiccup. As he points the half-emptied bottle of booze at Ophelia, he laughs. "Someone's got to around these parts."

Marinating on the man's inappropriate behavior, the Preacher surmises that the situation is spiraling out of control. Not knowing how to get Alonzo's attention, he leans over and grabs a clump of tousled hair peeking out from under his hat. "No, no, no. You can't just bat your eyes and guzzle down some of that bug juice. You're gonna get us both killed!" he says. Teetering at his wit's end, he casts aside his holy persona and dashes his hands through the air, grabbing at the drunk's bottle of booze.

The cowboy chuckles with each failed attempt at confiscation, taking another swig after every unsuccessful try. Sensing a drop of whiskey roll down his chin, he uses his shirtsleeve to wipe it away. "All right, Ophelia. Three!" he says.

He looks up at her foreboding position through glazed eyes. "Now, mosey on down here before I get too mopey off Kentucky's finest."

As soon as they make eye contact, her mouth unnaturally gapes open, revealing vomit-coated yellowed teeth severely decayed from enduring constant contact with stomach acid. Silence falls over the bar as she sucks in a massive inhalation of the room's frigid air, creating a sound like a wind tunnel. Without warning, her tongue protrudes from her mouth, and her throat releases a gravelly, demonic scream.

One by one, each of the candles blows out like a chain of tumbling dominoes. The Preacher keels over his knees and uses his hands to shield his eardrums from rupturing.

Alonzo Bill is unfazed by the racket. Removing his hat, he scratches his head, confused at how such a manly roar can come out of a girl so small. "Huh. Well, ain't that something?" he says.

Ophelia leans forward, and her body drops to the floor on all fours. Her limbs clatter against the floorboards, changing her previous leisurely stance, quickly carrying her body like a spider. In the blink of an eye, she scurries up the side of the stairwell's wall and disappears into the vaulted ceiling's dark abyss.

Certain the disappearing act is part of the performance, the cowman grows excited, and with the bottle wavering from the tips of his fingers, he scans the room to see where she went.

The quickening sounds of pitter-pattering feet nearby worry the Preacher. Sprinting to Alonzo, he grabs hold of his jacket, desperate to land his attention. His jittery eyes nervously scan each of the flameless candles. "You got to put down that prairie dew and do something before--" he says. Before he can finish his sentence, the sound of scampering ceases. His hands shake compulsively as he slowly shifts his gaze to the ceiling above them.

Alonzo's intoxication worsens with every passing second, and it delays his response in addressing the man's warning. Relaxed, a sizable open-mouthed smile settles with ease upon his lips. His pearly white teeth produce a smolder. Happily intoxicated, he stares directly into the eyes of the man gripping his lapels, and though drunk, he can still read the fear. "She's above me, isn't she?" Alonzo asks.

Petrified by what is transpiring overhead, the Preacher stutters and nods his head. "I-I reckon so," he responds.

"Did she crawl herself on up there all on her own?" Alonzo asks.

The Preacher drops his hands to his sides and trembles. He is terrified, but refrains from looking away. "I reckon she did," he says.

The cowboy is beside himself with incomprehension. Taking another swig from the whiskey, he shakes his head in disbelief and stares off into the distance. "Well, I'll be damned," he says.

His cavalier demeanor frustrates preacher Boone, and an expression of urgency falls over his face as he glares at the daydreaming alcoholic. His hand darts toward the bottle of whiskey, which is barely being held onto by Alonzo's fingers, and he snatches it away. "Gosh darn, you got to put that forty rod down, son, and listen!" he says, slamming the glass bottle against the bar. "This isn't the time to be befuddled!"

The sound of whiskey sloshing in the resting bottle grabs the cowhand's attention, but not for the intended reason, and his hands reach for the open container.

Suddenly, Ophelia falls from the ceiling, releasing demonic cackles as she lands like a graceful cat on the bar beside his yearning hand.

Without breaking eye contact with the crouching child, Alonzo slows down the pace of his retrieving hand, and as soon as his fingers wrap around the bottle, he rapidly retracts his arm. Mesmerized by her grossly disheveled appearance, he slowly sips from the bottle of whiskey like a zombie as he processes the unfolding scenario. "Preacher... what do you reckon we do now?" he asks.

Her father glances back to ensure nothing hides behind him, then quietly scoots away from the demonic stage.

Unable to take the anticipation any longer, Alonzo reluctantly breaks eye contact with the youngster.

Ophelia's mouth gapes open just as his head turns, and she projectile vomits, covering him in a waterfall of bright green bile.

Drenched in the foul-smelling sludge, he ceases all movement and freezes in disgust. Stuck in a moment of shock, he uses his fingers to wipe the bile from his eyes and sees Preacher Boone staring at him, petrified with fear.

Masking his changed perspective regarding the situation, Alonzo points to the green stain on the terrified father's shirt and makes light of the occurrence. "Guess that means she's smitten with us both now," he says with a tentative chuckle.

Overrun with terror, the Preacher neglects to join in the laughter. His legs tremble, his knees knock together, and the area around his pants' zipper grows wet with urine.

Ophelia mocks them from her crouching position with demonic growls and hissing lips.

Clenching his jaw, the cowboy turns to face the possessed child. His chest puffs confidently with liquid courage. As his skin heats from the whiskey, sweat builds underneath the bile. He reaches for the button on his collar to loosen it and, disgusted by a chunk of vomit on his shoulder, flicks the regurgitation off his shirt.

Thinking about her being the reason for his ruined shirt turns his face an angry red. He takes in a gulp of air to calm himself and glares at the perched child. "I bet you think this is funny, don't ya?" he says as he points to his soiled shirt.

Her face remains expressionless while she cocks her head to the side to observe him, and her demonic laughter escalates as her head tilts another degree to match his shifting pitch.

The Preacher opens his mouth to speak, and Alonzo immediately stops him. "Hush. Let me handle this," he says as he steps toward her. Relieved, the Preacher quickly nods and huddles on the floor.

As the cowhand approaches the bar, he rolls his sleeves to his elbows and drops his clenched fist to his sides. "Little girl, I will let you in on a secret," he says as he leans up against the bar. Looking into her eyes, he places each hand on the wooden edge and leans closer. "I've had women throw worse things at me, so your stunt doesn't have me balled up one bit."

Her tongue creates an inhuman ticking noise and sticks out as her hand violently pounds against the wood beneath her. Alonzo ignores her antics, turns his dismay into a condescending smile, and points to his face with seething anger. "Do it again, I dare you," he says.

Accepting the challenge, she lets out a guttural growl, releasing it through her gaping mouth.

Enraged with resentment from his ruined clothing, Alonzo lunges for a bottle glistening in his peripheral vision. Snatching what he believes is soda water from the shelf, he shakes it as if his life depends on it, then pops the cap so he can spray the contents into her eyes as a payback for the vomit. The bottle doesn't do what he predicted, as the water has no carbonation. "Ha!" he says as he covers his miscalculation and neurotically jiggles the open bottle of liquid at her, splashing it all over her face.

When the bottle's contents hit her skin, she lets out a deathly shriek and falls off her wooden stage to the floor. Her body convulses violently, and her eyes roll back into her head.

Her reaction leaves Alonzo confused, and he peers over the bar to look at her flailing body. His head snaps to the bottle in his hand that triggered the incident. Terrified of what may happen if he gets the liquid on his skin, he sets the bottle on the counter, wrapping his hand in a bar rag for protection. As the child wails in misery, he grabs the cap from the floor with the cloth and seals the bottle shut.

Distressed by his daughter's horrific wailing, the Preacher sprints to assist her. Setting his fear aside, he kneels on the floor beside her, repetitively whispering, "The Our Father," under his breath. His voice is overshadowed by her cries.

Still conflicted about the situation, Alonzo takes the bottle in his rag-protected hand and analyzes the label. Upon closer inspection of the black glass, he notices the writing has been smudged, and only a single gold cross remains.

The sound of Ophelia's screaming pulls him out of his deep contemplation. Worried he may miss the grand finale and forfeit pay for his services, he sets the bottle down and rushes to help. Almost too intoxicated to function, he braces his weight against the bar to stabilize himself and moves beside them, staggering.

The Preacher, hyper-focused on the frail child, escalates his voice, chanting prayers over the girl's flailing body.

Alonzo determines he is out of his element and awkwardly twiddles his thumbs. His eyes dart around the room as he watches the man delve deeper into the exorcism.

Motioning the sign of the cross into the air, the Preacher yells. "I banish the serpent from your body!"

Alonzo nods in agreement and mimics him with more extraordinary tenacity, not knowing what else to do. Hovering over them, he extends his hands over the duo. As his statuesque frame casts a shadow similar to the Messiah over the possessed child, the Preacher stops what he is doing and beholds the cowboy with admiration.

"Demon child, I banish the serpent from your body!" Alonzo shouts. Signing the cross dramatically in the air, he belches.

Ophelia's convulsions abruptly stop, and her body lays limp on the floor. As her father frantically scoops the dead weight of the child into his arms, her eyelids open, and she slowly wakes. She tries to orient herself to her surroundings as the lights in the saloon return to normal.

With tears welling in his eyes, Preacher Boone cradles her in a deep embrace. Groggily yawning, she asks. "Daddy? What happened?"

Overjoyed and in disbelief that his daughter is back to normal, the Preacher buries her face into his chest to keep her safe. "Nothing, my darling child. Everything is okay," he says. As he hugs her tightly, he peers up at the cowboy. "How-how did you..." he stammers.

Unable to wrap his head around the turn of events, Alonzo stands frozen in place, stunned by Ophelia's transformation. Slowly, he raises his hands to the level of his eyes and whispers to himself with a smirk. "There is nothing you can't do," he says.

The Preacher determines that his question is unimportant and directs his attention to his daughter. "I reckon I don't care how you got it done, just as long as my sweet Ophelia is back," he says.

Ignoring that he is puke-covered, Alonzo stands tall with a sense of accomplishment and answers the question. "Because I'm Alonzo Bill. Plain and simple."

Reaching for his coin pouch, he rolls a cigarette and lights it on the yellow flame of a reignited candle. He stares at his perfect reflection in a line of bottles on the other side of the bar. "I'm the best there is," he says as he inhales a cloud of nicotine and blows it into a smoke ring.

As he coughs lightly, he remembers the crazy series of events that just occurred, and is authentically spooked for the first time in his life. A creeping sensation rolls down his spine, his body shudders, and his glance darts to the black bottle sitting on the bar. The sight of the golden cross fills him with superstitious thoughts. Sure that it brought him good luck, he uses the rag to snatch it. "I'll be taking this one for the road, Preacher."

Still focused on the little girl's return, the Preacher lifts a hand to shoo the air. As he hugs her tighter in his arms, they cry.

Noticing the man is still distracted, Alonzo takes advantage of the opportunity to swindle more. With the bottle in hand, he walks around the bar and, using his empty palm, grabs an entire bottle of whiskey from the top shelf. "And this here, too," he says over his shoulder.

Complacently agreeing to his looting, the Preacher nods his head. He does not lift his eyes to acknowledge Alonzo honestly until he identifies the cowboy's footsteps growing heavier. As he regains his thoughts and composes himself, he eyeballs the cowboy, who's in a rush to leave. Hopping to his feet, he frantically rummages through the pocket of his pants and pulls out a handful of coins.

The sound of the clinking silver piques Alonzo's interest, and he turns around to look. The Preacher runs to catch up to him. "You know, I was wrong about you. Take anything you want. Heck, you can have all the free booze in this here saloon if it strikes your fancy. Truly, I owe you my life, and that of my daughter," he says as he places the handful of coins in Alonzo's palm. After his speech, the two men stand staring at each other in awkward silence.

Alonzo tries to hide the underlying terror lingering in his pupils. With his cigarette hanging from the corner of his lips, he shuffles the whiskey bottle under his arm so he can safely stow away the money in his pouch, then tips his hat to show thanks.

As he continues his path to the exit, he overhears the heartwarming reunion of the Preacher returning to his daughter, and he turns to take one last gander. Ophelia smiles with excitement and waves to the cowboy who saved her life. "Thanks, mister!" she says.

In acknowledgment, he smirks at the child. Refraining from getting choked up, he lifts his hand to adjust the brim of his hat and clears his throat. "Just another day in the life of a wrangler," he says.

As their joyous laughter returns, he exits into the desert sunrise.

Ten

Sure Is A Stupid Name

1869, Whittletown

The sun rises through groupings of cacti in the distance. Crows pillage for carcasses as the wind rolls across the desert floor, shifting the dug earth throughout the graveyard. Sweat caused by the laborious shoveling accumulates on the cowboy's dust-filled brows and drips down his five o'clock shadow. His tired hands lose steam as the exhaustion caused by the manual labor sets in and the alcohol dissipates from his system. Scooping up the last bit of ground left to fill the hole with one last heave, he flips the shovel over to pat the fresh soil. With the tilled sod packed tight, he takes a few steps back to admire his work.

Like sheep, you've come back to join me after all the hard work has been done. It's okay; I didn't need the help, anyway.

Wasn't that tale about the Preacher and his daughter a mighty fine story? That was the moment I became a full-fledged believer in spooky things. To this day, I carry that bottle of Jesus juice with me for good luck.

Yeah, I know. There is nothing poisonous about the bottle. It's holy water. I still don't know how it got on the saloon's liquor shelf, but one thing's for darn certain: it was meant for me.

After leaving the Preacher and his daughter, I headed to the local boarding house for the night, and while sitting alone in my room, I began inspecting the mysterious bottle. And I'll be damned if I didn't find, printed on the bottom of the container, the name of the place that blessed the contents, and looking for answers, I forged my path around, discovering its origin.

It led me up here, to this tiny, remote place they call Whittletown.

Reaching inside a hidden pocket within his jacket, Alonzo pulls out the black bottle with his bare hands and kisses the golden cross. He turns it upside down, surveying the engraving in the glass, and chuckles. "Whittletown," he says.

Placing the bottle back in his pocket for safekeeping, he carries the shovel over his shoulder as he wanders back to the steps of the small white church. He scans the structure as he enters, but not for bodies. "If I were a varmint, where would I keep my stash of firewater?"

Taking one last panoramic peruse of the building's interior, his pupils land on a stained-glass confessional sitting behind the altar. "Eureka. I just struck gold,"

Each piece of colored glass forming the ornate window of the sin-box door, shines like a cut crystal rainbow when hit by sunlight. The design showcases an overgrown field of ornate red flowers protected by thorns, and in between every twisting vine is a scripture of truth meant to cleanse the town of evil. All the intricate elements contradict the run-down exterior of the chapel.

As he admires the piece of art, Alonzo's throat pulses with aches. The outside elements have dried the cowboy's throat. Placing his free hand on his Adam's apple to provide relief, he swallows to cure the itch, and his desire overrides his patience. He makes his way to the altar and steps over the smeared blood on the aisleway floor. Arriving at his destination, he stops in front of the hand-carved altar and makes the sign of the cross before approaching.

He runs his fingers over its wooden surface, tracing the grooves of the pinewood knots stained with dried blood. "He was one bad man from Bodie ," he says.

Switching his focus, he walks over to the confessional with his shovel still in hand. Two doors sit side by side, one for the reverend's use, and one for his inferiors. Not putting much thought into which one to select, his fingers wrap around the knob on the right. Pulling the door open, he exposes the interior of the small bare room with a single wooden seat facing the shared wall.

The divider stationed between the two enclosures has a small sliding window built-in that resembles a food slot one might find in prison. Blanketing the interior's light-colored wooden walls on the sinner's side are etched names and the sins they committed. Some confessions seem frivolous, while others detail murders. An icy chill waltzes down Alonzo's back and leaves his mind with a sense of sorrow. Before removing his head from inside, he whispers a blessing. "Rest in peace," he says.

Still on a hunt for a drink, he tries to open the door on the Reverend's side and realizes it's locked. Analyzing the area around the handle, he catches sight of a hole suitable for a skeleton key. He glances at the graveyard waiting outside through the open doors of the chapel and kicks himself for not raiding the Reverend's pockets for the key before dumping him in the hole. Too tired to have any ambition, he uses the shovel to shatter the stained-glass window and reaches inside to unlock the door.

As the door creeps open, the small room's plush details become clear. Everything selected for decoration is lavish, with a rich velvet upholstered chair and silk curtains lining the walls. Alonzo's line of sight stops on the man's throne. A bottle identical to the one tucked in his jacket waits on the cushion. Snatching it from the red velvet, he pops off the top and holds the open bottle's neck under his nose. The smell of wafting moonshine puts a grin on his face. "That sneaky Devil," he says as he steps inside the confessional and sits on the expensive chair to rest.

As he sips on the homemade booze, he reflects on his journey.

Sitting in a box surrounded by everyone's dirty laundry hung out to dry makes a man's soul feel vulnerable. I've done some crazy stuff, but nothing compares to this. I hit the jackpot with this town, and believe me, it wasn't easy getting here. Encountering Preacher Boone's devil-filled daughter turned my world upside down and caused me to question what the hell I was doing with my life. I became a full-blooded believer of the unknown, denounced my con artist ways, and dedicated my life to ridding the world of mysterious evils. Hell, I even rediscovered my faith.

Over the next half a decade, I went against witchy things like werewolves, vampires, mischievous ghosts, and demonic spirits. Even though I knew my purpose, this little voice in my noggin wondered, why me? Why am I the chosen one?

From town to town, I would ask the villagers if they had tales regarding Whittletown, and everyone gave the same gawp of confusion until my last stop in El Paso gave me hope. There I was, up against a Chupacabra known for demolishing a fleet of cattle, and the rancher claimed to have traded stock with a farmer from the area. He warned me that something seemed off about the people, but I'm a selective listener.

The rest is history. I became like a mangy dog following a scent. After days of traveling, and divine intervention, I found Hell.

Buckle up, partners. I'm about to tell you the story, and you are in for one wild ride.

1869, Whittletown

The sound of his horse's hooves trotting against the packed dirt road brings life to the quiet terrain. A small white chapel sits on the right of the dusty path, surrounded by a freshly painted picket fence and a newly plowed garden.

Alonzo's clothing and tack ensemble contradicts the color of his steed. The stallion's hair is a delicate snow-white, and the saddle is crafted from pure black leather. He wears the finest of leather and suede to match the gallant richness of his hoofed transportation. Black chaps with silver metal decorations down each leg to hold the fringe in place match the black brushed-suede vest that covers his torso. Ostrich-skin boots with polished silver spurs spinning like tiny windmills adorn his feet. A stiff black cowboy hat sits on top of his head to protect the wrinkle-free skin on his face from the harsh elements. His choice of dark tones makes his ice-blue eyes glisten from the sun's reflection off the caramel desert land.

Peering toward the quaint church, he eyes a man wearing overalls with a red checkered shirt and straw hat painting the already-pristine white picket fence with what appears to be an identical white color. His eyes squint to get a better look. Digging his spurs into the stallion's ribs and with the reins in hand, he relieves tension on the horse's bit and instructs the creature to move in the direction of the chapel.

The man doesn't catch wind of the approaching steed and continues to paint. Every stroke of his brush is more frantic than the last.

With a quick tug on the bridle, the cowboy gets the beautiful creature to halt just a few feet away from the man's turned back. Not wanting to frighten the man, he gives the bridle a quick tug, triggering the horse to let out a playful introductory whinny. The man continues to ignore him, focused solely on painting the picket fence. Alonzo surveys the scene, waiting for acknowledgment, and finds it odd that there's not a bucket of paint in sight, only a man and a brush. Clearing his throat, he yells a friendly hello to address him. "Howdy there, Partner. Not trying to frighten ya, I just want to say hello and ask for some directions," he says.

The man's body tenses, stopping his paintbrush mid-stroke. With his back turned, he stays frozen in place, hunched over the fence for an awkwardly long time, standing in eerie silence.

The shift in energy causes the horse to rear and release a whinny that, unlike before, emits a tone of stress and fear. Alonzo knows something doesn't feel right about the mysterious man's behavior. Leaning forward over the saddle horn, he draws his body nearer to the stressed creature and gently extends his hand to rub the horse's muscular neck.

His eyes shift up. Peering between the horse's ears, he notices the man's head turning to the left at the speed of drying paint. His mind grows curious, and anticipation runs wild as he directs his full attention to the painter's turned back.

Every movement of the man's head appears out of sync with his neck and functions like an unoiled machine, as if each vertebra is disconnected from one another. His side profile reveals a ghost-white face with a single plastered-open eye. Sutures made from hay bailing twine lace his unopened eyelid shut, and the crude stitching spans the distance between his brow bone and cheekbone. Bruises surround the stitches, and bloodshot veins accent his remaining eye's iris-like crimson spider webs. His black-and-blue encircled mouth attempts to release words as his head turns, but the effort appears futile.

Alonzo winces at the sight of his gaping mouth exposing freshly plucked teeth and a removed tongue. Although the man's odd in appearance, he remains calm as he tries to give him the benefit of the doubt.

Without warning, the man charges his horse, and as Alonzo gets closer, he realizes that someone has permanently sewn the paintbrush into his hand. The sight is too much for Alonzo, and he throws his southern charm out the window. "Get a wiggle on!" he shouts. Spurring the horse wildly, it rears as if building momentum before lunging forward into a dead sprint away from the disturbing view.

He encounters a hand-painted wooden sign crudely hammered into the ground a short distance away. Not seeing any indication of the odd worker behind him, he pulls back on the reins, stopping to read the writing aloud. "Whittletown."

Taking off his hat, he wipes the sweat from his brow. Placing the accessory securely back on his head, he shields his eyes from the sun so he can better scan the horizon. "I'll be damned. I reckon we made it," he says as he lightly pats the horse's neck.

Standing before the duo is a town that appears frozen in time. Each building seems to be crafted with ordinary hands and each of them except the chapel is built in the style of identical rustic cottages. The main street appears deserted aside from herds of stray cattle roaming freely amongst the structures.

"Come on, let's explore," Alonzo says with a grin. The horse trills its lips and slowly walks.

Brushing off the image of the unsettling encounter from earlier, Alonzo straightens his posture, sitting tall on his steed. With each movement of the horse's hooves, his body sways in the saddle. The scenery triggers warm memories, reminding him of a small town near where he had spent his childhood. As he passes each building, he appreciates the well-kempt nature of the identically designed storefronts. Stopping in front of the leather shop, he peers through the plate-glass window at the plethora of cowboy hats on display.

A man dressed in overalls and a red plaid shirt resembling the attire of the rabid being from earlier spots the cowboy while cleaning a window. Alonzo aggressively rubs his eyes with his fists in disbelief over whether or not the man is wearing a similar outfit to the loon from earlier or if it's simply a mirage from his lengthy travels. The sound of a bell ringing from the store's door causes his eyes to open, and he discovers the man is real.

He pokes his head outside to wave to the out-of-towner. His smile is so big that it takes up half of his face and shows his off-white teeth. "I take it you are not from here," he says as his hand continues waving a mechanical hello.

The cowboy looks around to make sure he is talking to him and nods. "Mighty good guess. I was just passing through and thought I'd stop in," he says.

Lifting his finger in the air, the man motions for the cowboy to wait. He cautiously steps outside the storefront and quietly shuts the door behind him. Placing his hands in his overall pockets, he leisurely walks closer and lowers his voice. "What made you want to do that?" he asks.

The unwelcoming tone of the question throws him off. Adjusting his posture, Alonzo scoots himself to sit taller in his saddle. From the corner of his peripherals, he spots two more individuals peering out through storefront windows. Both are wearing identical overalls and a red-checked shirt ensemble, and he casually motions their way with a quick nod. "The better question is, what's up with the lunk-headed outfits?"

The man turns to get a better look at the peeping toms and chuckles. "Oh, well, reckon they do things differently here." The shopkeeper squints his eyes up at Alonzo.

"Could be," Alonzo says as the bystanders scurry away from their window. "I reckon you are the fourth I've seen wearing that combination."

Realizing the extent of the cowboy's curious nature, the man's cold demeanor shifts to a welcoming tone. "If I had to count, you've only seen three."

Before he can finish his rebuttal, the cowhand shakes his head. "Nope, I am certain it's four. That's counting the odd stick I ran into who was painting the church-looking building back there," he says.

The unidentified man scratches his head and peers in the chapel's direction. "I reckon they painted it sometime last week, so I can't think of who'd be painting it now. You must just be weary from your travels," he says.

Intent on proving the man wrong, Alonzo swivels in his saddle to survey behind him, but, after a long moment of observation, he sees no one there. "Huh," he says.

Taking advantage of Alonzo's distraction, the man quickly reaches into his pocket, pulls out a handful of locoweeds, and feeds it to the horse.

Alonzo snaps back around in a flurry when he hears his horse's nose let out a sneeze and witnesses the off-putting man petting his steed. Angry over his touching his faithful companion without permission, he shoots him a glare filled with skepticism.

Knowing that he almost got caught, the man shifts his demeanor from unwelcoming to one of jubilation. "I haven't seen one of these in ages. You know what? I reckon we got off to a poor start. Let's start again," he says. Before waiting for a response, he wipes his hand against his overalls and extends it to shake. "My name is Abraham, and that back there is my leather shop."

Alonzo stares at the extended hand from on top of the horse and keeps both palms wrapped around the carved handles of his colts. "Sure thing. I'm Alonzo. Alonzo Bill."

"Well, if you don't mind me asking. What do you do, Mr. Bill?" The man's pupils are abnormally large, and he stares blankly, refraining from a single blink while waiting for a response.

Clearing his throat to bide time, Alonzo brainstorms on the safest way to answer. "Just a traveling buckaroo," he says with a smile.

Abraham eyes up the horse and his expensive clothes. "Not used to one so rich. You appear like more of a barber's clerk to me," he says.

Alonzo shrugs his shoulders to act naïve. "What can I say? I guess I'm good at what I do." An unsettling feeling consumes his stomach, and he tugs on the reins for the horse to walk. "Well, as lovely as it was to make your acquaintance, I reckon I should be on my way before the sun sets."

The man scans off into the distance. "Shouldn't set for hours. It's only a hair after two," he says.

His odd mannerisms cause Alonzo's eyes to dart around the town in paranoia, scanning for an ambush. "I feel some barrel-fever coming on, so I'd best be on my way," he says. Unable to rid himself of the unsavory company fast enough, he presses his spurs into the horse's sides and is met with nothing but stagnancy from the creature. He slaps the end of his reins against its rump, and still, there's no movement.

He feels something is very wrong, but cannot pinpoint the cause of the animal's drastic change in behavior. No matter how hard he tries, the horse will not budge. While appearing concerned for the cowboy's stallion, the man's inner being diabolically calculates a plan. "Why don't you stay the day? It seems like both you and your horse need a little rest," he says.

The uncharacteristic nature of the stallion's idle state concerns Alonzo, but he has few options, and leaving the horse behind is not one of them. "I reckon a few moments won't hurt," he says as he dismounts his trusty steed.

Abraham smiles. "I reckon so," he says as he motions for him to follow.

Something about the tone of his reply causes Alonzo's shoulders to shudder. He tries to lead the horse and, finding his attempt unsuccessful, stretches the reins as far as they will reach and creates a loose knot, tying him to the shop's porch railing. Ensuring the stallion is secure, he surveys each end of the town's dusty street and realizes there is not a single pile of horse droppings. In fact, after thinking for a moment, he does not recall seeing a single equine. "Do y'all have a stable somewhere, or is it fine if he just rests here?" he asks.

"Everything is a close walk and easy to reach with two feet, so no one has the furry creatures here," Abraham says.

Glancing at the surrounding storefronts, Alonzo witnesses a small, identically dressed crowd gathering behind the windows to gawk at his horse. The men are garbed in overalls with red plaid shirts, and the women wear light-blue prairie dresses. "Whoever is selling the clothes to dress y'all must be rolling in *dinero*," he says.

The man picks up the pace of his feet and ignores his comment.

"You sure do things backward here," Alonzo says as he follows him inside the leather shop.

"Some may say that, but we refer to those as bad eggs," Abraham says with a shrug.

Growing distracted by the aesthetics of the row of cowboy hats, Alonzo shouts over his shoulder. "Bad eggs?" he asks.

"You know, bad eggs--nonbelievers who don't follow the word. They are all condemned to Hell, regardless, so the name ain't too important," he says.

The harsh words cause Alonzo's hair to rise on his neck. Swiftly, he changes the subject. "I see. So, what's the point of your shop if everyone wears the same outfit?" he inquires.

Brushing off the insult, Abraham shrugs and chuckles. "We allocate a day out of every month for wearing something new," he says.

Convinced the store must be a front to hide something peculiar, Alonzo pretends to take a gander at the hats while discreetly pushing on the walls to investigate for any hidden doorways. "Now that I think about it, I have another question for you," he says. With a flick of his wrist, he pulls the small black bottle from a hidden pocket inside his vest and extends the cross towards the shop owner.

The sight of the object makes Abraham's gaze grow wide, and he uses his hands to shield his eyes. "Where in God's name did you find that?" he asks. Frantically, he backs away, knocking over heaps of inventory in his terror-filled escape attempt.

Sounds of the bottle's sloshing liquid grow louder as Alonzo waves the half-full container directly in front of the man's covered eyes. "Whoa, now, partner. You didn't even let me finish," he says.

"Finish your asking; just please, put that away," Abraham says while covering his eyes.

Alonzo carefully tucks the bottle back into his vest with a smirk. "All right, you can look now. It's gone," he says as he chuckles.

Peeling his fingers away from his eyes, Abraham hesitantly peeps, and noticing it's gone, exhales a sigh of relief.

Walking across the store, Alonzo grabs a lonely apple sitting on the storekeeper's desk and takes a huge bite. "Why the sour face?" he asks mid-chew.

The man is ghostly pale and still spooked by what he had seen. "Yo-you don't even know what you are holding close to your heart," he says as his shaking finger points to his vest.

Alonzo finds the theatrical performance comical. "All I got is the Lord's water," he says. Finishing the apple, he throws the core onto the floor.

The man anxiously shakes his head. "No, you don't understand. Only the Reverend is allowed to touch those bottles," he says. "If we ever were to get close to one, it would land us the noose."

"I reckon he sounds like my kind of man," Alonzo says. Growing excited, he paces the store. "When can I meet him?"

Abraham freezes in place, becoming mute as he attempts to articulate a complete sentence. His voice stutters. "Only members of our community may see him in the flesh," he says.

"That don't work for me," Alonzo says as he shakes his head. "I reckon after hearing your warnings, I have to meet the man who runs this shindig."

The terrified man's teeth chatter. "I'll see what I can do," he says as his eyes scan the room for eavesdroppers.

The words are music to Alonzo's ears, and at the moment's excitement, he walks across the room and slaps the man on his back. "That's what I like to hear!" he says. As he sarcastically chuckles, he leans closer to whisper. "And thank God no damage was done, but if I catch you trying to feed my stallion locoweeds again, I'll skin your body alive and hang your carcass to dry in the desert," he says. Laughing, he swats Abraham's back harder than the time before.

He gulps at the threat and silently nods.

Lifting his hand, Alonzo acts as though he is preparing to whack him again. "Now scram, before I decide to be less forgiving," he says.

Before he can finish his threat, the store owner runs toward the door. "Whoa, partner!" Alonzo says as he draws the pistol from his holster and, with a steady hand, points the loaded gun at the fleeing man.

As the hammer clicks into place for the shot, the owner slowly puts his hands in the air and turns to face the cowboy, who motions for him to come closer. He leaves his hands in the air and cautiously approaches, following his direction.

The cowboy snaps the fingers of his free hand and points to his pocket. "Now, how am I supposed to trust you after you already tried to pull the wool over my eyes?" he says.

The act of staring down the barrel of a loaded gun panics Abraham. "Whatever you want me to do, I'll do it," he says.

"Go on now, reach into your pocket," Alonzo says. Irritated by his lack of listening, he wiggles the gun to threaten him. "Now!"

"OK, just please don't shoot." Slowly, he lowers his right hand into the opposite pocket.

Alonzo points with the gun in his hand to the opposite one. "The other one."

Following his command, Abraham reaches into the opposite pocket and feels the locoweeds under his fingertips. "I want to see what you are hiding there," Alonzo says.

Abraham's trembling hand pulls out the handful of poisonous plants to show the cowboy.

The sight makes him smile. "Now, put them in your mouth," he says. The man's hesitancy makes Alonzo angry, and he shoots a bullet at his feet.

Abraham jumps with fear and shoves the plants into his mouth, closing his eyes.

Alonzo leaves his pistol drawn and walks closer to watch him. "Now swallow!" he says through his gritting teeth. "Open your mouth." Seeing the remnants are gone, he fires another shot at his feet. "I'd get a wiggle on before that kicks in."

The man frantically turns around and sprints to the door.

Alonzo fires a single shot into his back, grinning as he collapses to the floor, then walks over and kneels beside him. Checking for signs of life and finding none, he glances up from the body and discovers that the noise of gunfire has caused a crowd to build outside. Rising to his feet, he steps to the open entrance. "Go on, git!" he yells. As the town members disperse, he shouts another threat from the open shop door. "Tell the head honcho I'm here to see him, and I won't stop killing until I do."

Stepping outside, he unties his horse and places his head on its forehead. Looking into his eyes, he recognizes that the effects of the locoweed have waned. "Get far away from here and don't come back. Do you hear me? This is it."

Quickly, he removes the steed's saddle and bridle. Slapping its behind, he fights back his emotions. "Git!" he says.

The horse gallops into the far distance until it is no longer visible.

Alonzo retreats inside the shop and locks the door. Glancing down at the corpse, he chuckles as an idea comes to mind. He grabs hold of a foot and drags the body through the shop until he reaches the display window. Propping him up behind the plate glass, he places a hat on his head. "Come on now, don't look blue. It ain't all bad, partner. At least you can finally enjoy the finer things more than once a month," he says.

Finished arranging the windows' display, he retreats to the corner of the store to sit behind the clerk's counter with his pistol in hand. Leaning back in the chair, he puts his boots on the countertop and waits for the Reverend. "I reckon he messed with the wrong buckaroo."

Eleven

Bad Man From Bodie

Night sets through the town. Trying not to drift off, Alonzo shifts positions to stay awake. Staring at the locked door of the hat store, he smirks as his eye line moves to the man lying dead in the display window.

I tell you, it's a dog-eat-dog world out there, and I'm just living in it. After killing that man, I hope you don't feel I have pulled the wool over your eyes regarding my trustworthy demeanor. He had it coming.

I think it is only fair that I level with all of you on some things. At one point in my life, I may or may not have been considered a Bad Man from Bodie. Rather than refer to that time as turmoil, I prefer to explain it as a trial that got me to where I am.

While waiting for this Reverend to show his pretty little face, I'll shed some light on my past. Trust me, it wasn't all peaches and cream. There's a lot I'm not proud of, but it made me tougher than nails.

1845, Bodie

As a cowboy without a pot to piss in, he's stuck like most supplementing his earnings by working in the mines. It isn't easy to make a single cent living that life. Night after night, he would fight for a piece of bread and a bed to sleep in.

Stumbling upon the town that promised gainful employment, Alonzo feels hope for once in his life. He could make a decent living rather than living his life as a cowhand, and for that, he's grateful. With inexperienced eyes, he stumbles onto the desolate land with an open mind and a stained knapsack stuffed with a single day's worth of clothes.

A man with a rugged gray beard greets him and laughs at his naïve demeanor. "You sure you're cut out for this work?" he asks.

The cowboy's baby face nods. "I'll work as hard as needed, as I need payment," he says.

The man pats him on the back. "In that case, my name is Kit, and this here is the town of Bodie," he says as he points to the desolation.

Alonzo's eyes grow wide with endless possibilities as he surveys the terrain.

"You got any kin?" Kit asks.

"Nope, my momma died early on."

"Well, that works well in this line of work. Many accidents happen in these mines, and I don't want to be liable for notifying someone's family."

The doe-eyed cowboy nods in agreement. "Sure."

"Well, come on and follow me then," he says as he starts the tour. Intrigued by all the amenities, the young cowhand follows along.

Walking down the dirt path, Kit motions to the melting snow. "During the winters, it can be a little brutal, but you won't have to worry about too much since y'all will be spending most of your time below ground."

Without looking behind him, he continues to walk and points to a building with swinging wooden panel doors. Light peers from the top and bottom of the hinged wings. Pointing to it, he continues. "That there is the local drinking hole," he says.

The commotion inside intrigues the cowboy's youthful innocence, never having seen the inside of a bar before. Kit notices the boy's stagnancy, and he stops and turns to face him. "Oh, boy, don't tell me you're new to the life."

The boy shakes his head to cover his hide. "No, sir," he says.

Chuckling at his response, Kit continues down the road to the mining hole. Reaching a boulder formation, he points to a jagged railway sticking out. "Well, this is it. This is where you show up when the sun rises." Lifting a hand, he turns to face him. "Honest to God, the harsh winter made us lose a few more men than we planned, so as long as you wake up and show up, you'll be okay," he says.

The youthful cowhand nods as he listens. "Yes, sir."

"If you want to survive here, you got to stop that. Polite will only get you killed," he says while observing the gun holstered to the cowboy's hip. The old man appears defeated, and switches his exhausted demeanor to a cheerful one. "Let's drink to celebrate."

The innocent boy's eyes light up with a hefty nod.

Retracing their steps, they walk back to the local saloon they passed earlier. As they enter through the swinging doors, everyone greets the mountain-looking man. He acknowledges them by nodding, pulls a stool out for the new hire, and orders them each a drink.

Still a bit reserved, Alonzo nervously takes the whiskey and drinks a sip. "It's good, ain't it?" Kit asks. The anxious cowboy smiles and nods.

As fast as that life started, I got caught up in the darkness, and booze became my downfall. Spending each paycheck on my bar tab, I would get involved in some dark shit, and I'm not proud, but that includes killing. Men would mosey into town to pick a fight, and I would defend my honor. It was my past and the only way to survive.

The work gave me a living to put a roof over my head. Still, I remember a trivial time when I didn't like the man I had become, and to this day, it sends a shudder down my spine. I would routinely involve myself in bar fights and wake up from my blacked-out state in a confused daze, but as long as I performed my job, everyone condoned my behavior, and like a cock fight, I reckon many got weekend entertainment from it.

One morning, after a night of too much whiskey, I showed up late to work, and that was when it all changed.

As Alonzo enters the mining hole, the air blows cold as ice, and the walls are damp with dew. His eyes are bloodshot from a late night at the bar, and his left eye is blackened from a questionable altercation he could not recall. Even with his turbulent trials and errors, he's still showed up, albeit late, to perform the harsh manual labor.

Waiting in line with the rest of the men, he grabs his pickax to begin his excavation for treasure. He follows behind the crew, only to discover that his regular spot has been taken by a new employee who got there before him.

Alonzo pounds on the harsh wall throughout the day, but unlike the times before, he finds no luck around him. Each time the new fellow's name is cheered beside him for his success, he tastes defeat. "Zeke, Zeke, Zeke!" the workers call.

The words echo through the tunnels, and Alonzo, consumed by the green-eyed devil, grows ill with envy. He hits the unforgiving stone wall more aggressively than before. As the rock tumbles to his feet, he scrambles to the ground to sift for signs of gold, but is left only with treasureless disappointment. Sitting on the dampened floor, he pouts as he stares at the new hire and kicks the dirt in frustration.

I would have gotten his spot in line if I weren't out bending my elbow. I bet he couldn't tell skunks from house cats if he tried.

Believing that good luck is owed to him for being employed for a longer time, Alonzo's entitlement causes him to attempt to reduce the new hire's success through passive means. Standing to his feet, he rants and raves, kicking the wall. "Blam-jam!" he says. His failure and others' success bring resentment to his blood.

Zeke hears the commotion and turns to face him. His dirty, mousy brown beard trails down to his belly button with specks of debris intermixed in the unkempt mess. Dressed in variations of light brown, it is difficult to tell if the color is original or the clothes are dirty. He laughs at the muddy mustard boots and dark brown suspenders of the man throwing a hissy fit next to him. "I'd cool down if I were you, son. You're acting crazier than a rabid raccoon," he says.

The surrounding miners, covered in smudged dirt, stop their work to join in his mocking. Their cackling laughter grows louder in the tunneling cave.

Alonzo's face becomes red with festering hate, and the atrocious sounds of jeering create irritating stings that penetrate his ears. His vision blurs. Clenching his fists, he turns to face the taunting crowd and focuses specifically on the bearded man's tobacco-stained toothless smile. "What did you say, old man?" he asks.

Getting a kick out of his riled-up demeanor, the group grows louder with egging calls. A man wearing patched-together clothes and torn knickers steps forward next to Zeke. As he wails with laughter, his dust-layered face with scruffy brows contorts into a large Jack-o-lantern smile, showing his broken teeth with black streaks. "I reckon you should clean his plow," he says, nudging Zeke's arm.

Zeke glares down at the hunchbacked, decrepit mountain man and howls with laughter. Feeling cocky, he joins in and nudges him back. "Cast your eyes on him. I reckon his family tree was a shrub, and his momma a shrub-dwellin squirrel," he says.

As everyone laughs louder, Alonzo's fist clenches tighter around the handle of his pick. "Keep my poor momma out of this. I'm warning you," he says.

Wanting to witness a fight break out, the group of the foul-tongued, torn-clothed workers encourages the new worker to tussle. As the raucous cheering builds, a lanky man with a missing eye emerges to speak up. His mustache is a stained strawberry blonde color, and his features are pointed like a weasel's. His dark blue work pants are ill-fitting, with one leg hiked six inches too high and the other six inches too long. "I reckon I wouldn't do that if I were you, Zeke," he says.

With the pickax in his hand, Alonzo turns to see who is speaking, and recognizing the injured man, he grins. "Well, howdy there, Bill. That eye sure is healing up nice," he says.

The man glares at him. Turning to the crowd, he points at his missing eye and the singled-out man mocking him. "He may not come across as much, but that son of a gun is so mean he'd eat rattlesnakes for breakfast, and I'm proof. He took my one good seeing eye," he says.

Everyone gasps and looks at Zeke, curious about what he will do. "I got to side with the boogered-up man," Alonzo says.

Zeke puffs out his chest and grins with a confident smile as he believes his masculinity is being questioned. "Oh yeah? Well, I reckon I could take you," he says.

Holding onto his britches, Alonzo burrows into the crowd of men.

Without warning, Zeke yells at the top of his lungs like a warrior's cry and charges at the young, lean cowboy.

As Alonzo patiently waits, his grip adjusts to secure itself on the wooden handle of his pickaxe. Swinging the weapon wildly, his vision darkens as his aim becomes more purposeful. He aims the sharp edge of the forged spike at the bear of a man, and with a single blow, a huffing sound exudes from the man's lungs as the pointed ax lodges into his gut. Blood spatters the room and across the cowboy's face. His tongue licks a droplet from his lips, and a crazed frenzy takes over.

Holding his abdomen, Zeke falls to his knees. Lifting his ax into the air, Alonzo leaps on top of him and swings with all his might.

The crowd becomes wild with excitement, and they circle the duo to get a better view of the carnage.

Even though the man is unconscious, Alonzo's rage spirals out of control, and every ounce of anger from his hard life translates through his fists.

As the man lays dying on the floor, a gurgle leaves his nostrils, and his limbs fall limp.

Still unsatisfied, Alonzo grabs a clump of the man's beard to steady his head. "You are as ugly as homemade sin," he says. Using the blade of the pick, he grits his teeth and scalps Zeke, smirking with deep fulfillment as he watches the skin of the man's head fall to the floor. He stands to look at the bystanders and holds out the tip of his ax to see who wants to be next.

They jump with fear and disperse faster than a sandstorm.

Wiping the blood away from his face, he chuckles at their terror. "That's what I thought," he says as he makes his way to a wooden cart holding nuggets of gold. His hands take as many as he can carry. As he hides them in his pockets, he glances at the mangled body on the floor. Unlike his prior altercations, the gruesome sight causes a tinge of guilt to invade his heart.

"I'd get gone if I were you. I reckon you may receive the California Collar for that one," Bill says from a distance away.

Even though the man is unreliable, Alonzo knows his lawless behavior may catch up to him, having left so many witnesses. Looking at the body, he gives one last remark. "I remember little of my family, but my momma did the best she knew how," he says as he points his finger to scold Zeke.

Letting out a grunt, he runs out of the mine as fast as his feet can carry him and doesn't look back.

1869, Whittletown

When they say I never looked back, let me tell you, I never did. The town doesn't exist anymore. But that day, I fled from the town of Bodie with only the gold in my pockets and clothes on my dirty skin. To this day, I still remember hearing the screams of a woman and children in the distance behind me as I hit the outskirts of that town. Even though I couldn't see their faces, I knew deep in my gut it was his family finding out the dreadful news.

That was a pivotal moment for me, and served as a wake-up call for my violent ways. Even though it didn't pay as well, I used the treasure I'd confiscated to start a new life as a cowboy. I had a clean slate. Well, from violence. I still got into some sin, but more of the womanizer type. I'm a good-looking cowboy, so it comes with the territory, along with the occasional fistfight.

He yawns, causing his eyelids to grow heavy with exhaustion. "I suppose a little snooze won't hurt," he says. Gazing through the plate glass window to the pitch-black terrain outside, the sleepiness overtakes him, and he snores, cuddling with the cold metal of the pistol.

Twelve

No Sleep For The Wicked

is snoring sounds like the snorts of a tiny piglet, and his lips whistle with each exhale. Aggressive knocking echoes from the glass of the storefront's window. The jarring noise causes Alonzo to spring awake from his slumber, causing the cowboy hat shielding his eyes to fall to the floor. His fingers fumble for his pistol while his other hand draws the second one from the opposite carved-leather holster on his hip. He yawns as his blurry eyes focus on the cause of the pounding.

A crowd of angry town folk waits outside with pitchforks and flaming torches. Noticing a stirring commotion from inside the leather shop triggers their shouting lungs to project louder. "Alonzo Bill! Alonzo Bill! Alonzo Bill!" they shout.

Gathering his bearings, he uses the end of the pistol to scratch his head and leans over to fetch his cowboy hat from the floor. "How in God's gravy do those loons know my name?" he says. Using the barrels of the guns like tongs, he places the hat on his head and points his weaponry at the crowd. He cautiously approaches them, shouting loudly enough for them to hear him through the glass. "You bring that nasty Reverend with you?" he asks.

Ignoring his request, they pound harder on the window. "He who kills has no free will!" they chant. A group of women wearing blue prairie dresses and with their hair tucked in bonnets hisses at the dead body in the window.

His attention shifts to each of their middle-aged faces. "Jesus, those hens are wilder than feral cats," he says. He turns to address the fanatical pack. "Suppose I don't go. What then?"

One by one, the citizens take turns beating the glass. "I reckon with a crazy wild ass glass pounding response like that, its best I don't go nowhere with y'all," he says.

"Burn, burn, burn!" they shout. A group of men in matching overalls and identically slicked hair move to the front of the group with torches.

Alonzo's eyes grow expansive at the sight of the flames. Waving the silver guns through the air, he sprints to the front door to get them to stop. "Whoa, now! Don't got to tell me twice! I'm coming out," he says.

As he takes a deep breath, he stares up at the sky. "Lord, if you protect me from those inbred fools, I promise: no more sin for me." Lowering his pistols to his holsters, he reluctantly unlocks the door.

The townspeople flood in like a high tide from a polluted sea and swarm around him.

A small boy with an unusually prominent forehead runs inside to the window display as they try to restrain him. His overalls match the others, but his shirt is blue plaid instead of red. "Father!" he shrieks. He crawls through the display of hats, knocking inventory to the floor. Reaching the window display, he climbs on top of the corpse. "No!" he says, with tears streaming down his face.

A young woman runs to his side. "Don't cry, little Tom. That man is not your father; it's only a shell, nothing more. You got to remember what the Reverend said," she says.

The child sniffles and nods. Slowly backing out of the display, he locks eyes with Alonzo. "You're a bad man, mister."

Alonzo fixates on the child's outlandish forehead as he fights the men restraining his arms. "I may be bad, but I am not as ugly as a skunk. I've been wondering, does that thing make you smarter than the others??"

More gruff men wearing identical overalls circle him, grabbing his feet. Lifting him off the floor, they carry him like a hammock out the shop's door. As his body swings side to side, dust from the men's shuffling boots kicks up into his eyes.

He winces and sneezes. "Now, I'm not complaining about the royal treatment, but could y'all watch your feet. I got allergies to dirt, and this dust is causing a deep itch in my nose," he says.

Tired of his remarks, an ogre-statured man walking beside them takes a used handkerchief out of his pocket.

The cowboy catches sight of the red paisley pattern dancing through the wind towards his face and turns his head away in disgust. As he smells the unwashed material approaching closer, he shuts his mouth and holds his breath. His fighting limbs cause the group to pause, and the man makes his way to the other side of his body.

Unable to control himself, the cowboy lets out a sneeze. Using his dirty fingers, the man stuffs the booger cloth inside his gaping mouth to quiet him. While laughing with an oddly high pitch like a toddler, he hovers over the cowhand's panicked eyes and refrains from moving.

A man with a curled gray mustache adjusts his grip on the cowboy's left foot to yell at the man-child. "Okay, John, now go on, git! You are holding us up, and he's getting mighty heavy," he says.

Alonzo's eyes shift to observe the family drama unfolding. Out of spite, he snatches the cowboy hat from the vigilante's head and puts it on. He stares, pouting at the scorning man.

"Don't make me hand you over to the Reverend," he says. Taking the hat, John pretends to be riding a horse and gallops away to the back of the group.

The mustached man appears stressed as he eyes John. "Should have listened to the Reverend when that child was born an odd stick," he says.

All the men holding on to the cowhand nod in agreement. "He's always right," they say.

Alonzo rolls his eyes in disbelief. With each step, his body swings like a pendulum, and he finds the rocking motion calming. Looking at the star formation above, he can tell they are heading toward the small chapel he had passed earlier. Shutting his eyes to pass the time, he attempts to make use of the situation to rest, getting some shuteye to recharge for whatever is about to happen next.

The further they walk, the more fatigued the men hoisting his body's weight become, and his britches begin to drag on the ground. The sting of a rug burn forming on the seat of his pants triggers his eyes to leap open. Scanning the scenery above, he recognizes they are close to their destination, and the sound of the picket fence creaking open confirms his assumption.

The rest of the townspeople tentatively wait behind the picket fence and do not enter the holy ground. With wide eyes, they stare at the men transporting the intruder. With three loud thuds, the four men finish dragging his body up the church's steps to the front door. Each of the men trembles as they look at each other for what to do next.

"I reckon you should open the door," the man with the handlebar mustache says to the two men closest to the entrance.

As they fight over who should be the first to enter, a grating sound echoes from the rusted hinges as the door opens unprovoked. In unison, all the men's faces turn ghostly white as they peer inside. "I don't want to go in there. Y'all heard what happened to Levi," the man holding his right arm says.

Still restrained, Alonzo is helpless. All he can do is wait like a sitting duck for his fate to be presented.

The sound of a loud gunshot resonates from the church. As Alonzo's nostrils breathe in the aroma of fresh gun powder, his eyes dart in the noise's direction. His right arm falls, hitting the planks of the wooden porch as the man who was just talking falls limp to the ground.

The other three gawp at their dead brother, then stare at one another with panic. Just as the man with the well-groomed mustache opens his mouth to speak, three more shots ring out like church bells on a Sunday morning.

The men release the cowboy's limbs without warning, and he falls flat on his back as their bodies fall to the ground around him one by one.

He rips the stuffed hanky from his mouth and spits out the foul taste. Stunned by the turn of events, he sits up with his back to the doorway, and his eyes dart to each of the dead bodies.

A voice echoes from the dark interior of the church. "Come hither, my child." The sound of the mysterious voice makes the hairs stand on the back of his neck. Alonzo turns his body and peers through the entrance of the chapel to investigate the darkness. "I've been waiting for you," it says.

Lifting his hand, he looks at the corpses and, in confusion, points to himself. "Yes, you. Don't worry about those buffoons. I've wanted them gone for a while."

"Don't blame you," Alonzo says as he stands to his feet and nervously laughs. Taking a few steps forward, he enters the church and spots the outline of a medium-statured man standing at the altar, praying over a body. The door loudly shuts behind him, and he jumps. His mind runs wild. *It's just the wind.*

The figure raises his hands to give an offering to God and releases a deep laugh. Without looking, he summons Alonzo. "Come closer."

Brushing the dirt from his pants, he clears his throat and does a slow processional down the narrow aisle between the pews. "I take it you're the Reverend I've been looking for."

The figure's head snaps up to look at the disheveled cowhand as the words resonate between the walls. "I reckon you are smarter than you look," he says.

A mask made of horsehair covers the man's face. Each lock has been matted together and laced with burlap rope.

The ornate stitchwork resembles the craftsmanship Alonzo had seen used on the mysterious painter. Small slits provide holes for his eyes, and one that is a bit larger sits over the center of his lips so he can speak. Squinting through the shadows, he sees that the man is draped in a long black clergy robe with a hood, further concealing his identity. "It must be hotter than Hell underneath that thing," he says.

The Reverend ignores the unenlightened comment and continues with his blessing. Placing his hands amongst a nondescript heap, he casts his eyes to the heavens. "I offer this to you, Lord, Father of all that is good and slayer of all that is evil. Deliver us from eternal damnation," he says as his hand motions the sign of the cross.

Uncomfortable with the bizarre situation, Alonzo scans from side to side, looking for an excuse to change the subject. A shiver falls over his body, and he crosses his arms to warm himself. "It's awful chilly in here. I can help you fix whatever crack is causing that draft," he says.

The Preacher lifts his hands higher into the air and speaks louder for all to hear. "In the name of all that is powerful, I condemn the evil out of his soul and the feast to begin," he says.

Taking a few more steps, Alonzo flinches at another wave of the icy breeze hitting his skin. This time, a wafting stench smelling of rot travels with it. "Jesus Christ, Preacher, what in the Hell is that Godawful stench?" he asks as he waves the air away from his nostrils. Making it to the altar, he gets a clearer view of what's causing the permeating smell, and he uncontrollably folds to dry heave.

A dismembered town member's remnants rest in a rotting heap on top of the altar. Each limb has been hacked and intermixed with entrails, skin, and bone. A severed hand with a paintbrush sewn to it hangs off the altar.

Alonzo gives himself a mental pep talk to rid himself of nausea. Compartmentalizing the stench by remembering when he would shovel cattle dung and spread manure, he takes a deep breath and picks his body up from his knees. The black-and-blue decayed fingers attached to the paintbrush meet his first glance. The familiarity intrigues him, and he analyzes the rest of the body parts to place his recognition. He freezes on the decapitated head.

Though the spark in the corpse's single remaining eye has vanished, it remains fixed open with the sutured stitching made of hay bailing twine. The toothless and tongueless mouth has also been stitched to stay open, and vital organs fill the gaping void.

Alonzo realizes it is the same man he had spotted painting the fence earlier and cringes. "He's real after all. If that's not reassuring, I don't know what is," he says as he scratches his head. Trying to process the gruesome scene, he turns to the front row of worn wooden pews and takes a seat.

The Reverend's eyes roll into his head, and with only the whites of his eyes visible, they appear to glow. Speaking in tongues, he slams his fists against the sacrificial blood-soaked butcher block. Then, hunched over the remains, he sticks his tongue through the slit of the mask and, with a moan, licks the rotting flesh. Like a hog eating from a trough, he wriggles his face in the gore until he frees a piece of flesh with his teeth. With cannibalistic prowess, he chews and chews the putrid skin.

Swallowing the carnage, he stands upright, looking directly into the observing cowboy's confused eyes. "Sometimes I forget my manners," he says as he extends the corpse's decomposing foot to him. "Would you like a taste?"

Alonzo adjusts his position on the unforgiving wooden pew to obtain comfort. He winces while politely waving a hand to decline the offer. "I am as full as a tick," he says.

The cloaked man shrugs and continues to feast on the rotting body. With a full mouth, he continues to speak. "Did you have a comfortable trip?" he asks.

Trying not to peer directly at the cannibalism, Alonzo runs his fingers through his hair and turns his head towards the sparsely placed darkened windows. "It was pretty relaxing until an odd stick snatched the hat right off my head," he says.

"That's a mighty pity. Would you like me to call someone to fetch it for you?" the cloaked man asks.

As he lifts his blood-stained hands to aid his yell, the cowboy gets an image of John's squalid hair leaving greasy stains on the interior and motions him to stop. "Don't bother. I was fixing to get a new one, anyway," he says.

Wanting to get the show on the road, he leaps to his feet and pulls the black bottle from inside his vest. "Let's cut to the chase."

The sight of the black bottle with the gold cross emblem catches the leader's attention, and he perks up. Finishing his bite, he returns the foot to the table and puts all his focus on Alonzo. "You've caught my attention," he says.

Sensing he may finally get some answers regarding the origination of the mysterious bottle excites him, and he approaches the altar. "Good. So, tell me about this here elixir," he says. His pupils try to decipher the cloaked man's facial expressions, but the mask makes it impossible.

As the cowboy approaches, the clergyman paces, "Tell me, how did you find it, or should I say how did it find you?" he asks.

Holding the bottle, Alonzo frustratingly throws his hands into the air. "Come on now, don't do this back-and-forth shit with me; I don't got time for it," he says. Angry, he shoves the tinted glass in the man's face.

"It's quite simple. It was put in your path to call you home," the cloaked man says with a cynical cackle.

"Home?" he asks.

The leader walks the altar as if giving a sermon. "You see, all of our children return eventually," he says.

Irritated by being lumped together with the weirdos of the town, Alonzo's face gets red, and he interjects. "I'm not one of your screwballs," he says through his gritted teeth.

"Are you certain of that?" the Reverend responds with an unnerving snicker. Like declaring an offering to the Lord, he exaggeratedly raises his hand and points to Alonzo's chest. "How'd you get that scar on your chest?"

Placing the bottle back in his vest, Alonzo's hands jump to his shirt to check if it's unbuttoned. Realizing each of the buttons is securely fastened, he turns to face the cynical being. His eyes grow skeptical as he tries to figure him out. "What else do you know?" he asks, while his hand rests on the gun's handle in his holster.

The man's tempo becomes condescendingly unhurried as he slowly takes a deep breath of the rotten air and closes his eyes. "If you kill me, you won't learn where you came from, my boy."

The expression, typically used by a father, stops Alonzo in his tracks. He thinks about the repercussions of killing the only potential he has left to learn about his past. Reluctantly, he retracts his clenched hand from the pistol. His expression turns cold as ice. "I'm not your boy!"

The cloaked man notices him swirling in confusion and changes the trajectory of the conversation, giving him what he seeks. "Listen to your heart," he says as his bloodstained hand reaches out to touch the cowboy's chest.

As the man's fingers contact the area of his scar, a widespread shock runs through Alonzo's body, overwhelming him. He feels as though a ton of black coal has smothered his heart. He is not fond of dealing with his repressed emotions, and lifts his right hand to slap the Reverend's touch from his chest.

With a flick of his wrist, the leader telepathically ushers his hand to his side. "Don't fight it.

Acknowledge and feel what is trapped inside, and you shall be cleansed," he says.

Alonzo tries with all his strength to lift his hand, but a mysterious force holds it back. Panic pervades his eyes, causing his vision to become foggy. His legs collapse from underneath him, and he tumbles to the floor. Drifting into an incoherent state, he can hear the Reverend's voice.

"You shall be cleansed; you shall be cleansed; you shall be cleansed."

Relinquishing control, Alonzo feels his mind start to lose its grip.

Dang, it's gonna be a long ride. Here we go.

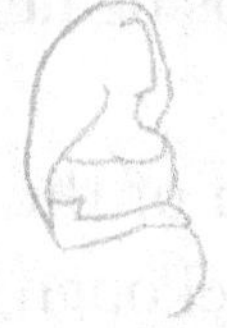

Thirteen

The Chosen One

1825, Whittletown

Wild horses run freely between the stray cactus formations surrounding the remote town. A young barefoot woman walks carefully down the dirt road, avoiding pebbles in her path. Her features are petite, hazel-colored eyes are shaped like almonds, and her hair is a chestnut brown. As her long floral-patterned prairie nightgown flows in the wind, the outline of her enormous belly shows.

She is exhausted. Her anxious pupils contradict her cheerfully humming a tune. Taking a few more steps down the isolated road, she hears the boisterous sound of a sermon being given by her husband to the townsfolk coming from a newly built, unpainted chapel. His voice causes her posture to stiffen.

Bells sound from the top of the shed-like structure, echoing through the isolated civilization. The sound causes her feet to stop and her core to be paralyzed with fear. She neurotically rubs her belly to feel the fetus kick. "Hush, little one. It will be okay. I will keep you safe," she says, closing her eyes to inhale a deep breath.

The ominous groan of the chapel door opening causes her eyes to peel open with paranoia. One by one, the villagers exit the church with uniforms in hand--long prairie dresses for the females, pink for the little girls and blue for the women, and overalls for the males, with red-checkered shirts for the men and blue-checkered for the boys. Everyone appears defeated as they stare at the ground, mourning the loss of their individuality.

After the last citizen exits the structure, the Reverend follows behind and stands on the porch to admire his followers. Rather than wearing a clergy cloak, he prefers a traditional preacher's collar, allowing his expression to be seen. The features set on his face are robust, and his jawline is chiseled. Above his stubbled cleft chin and Grecian nose sit a pair of icicle-blue eyes. His blonde locks are perfectly styled. "Remember, if you are down, pray about it. We must give up all our worldly possessions. This is what the Lord commands!" he says as he rests his back against the raw wood shingles on the porch of the chapel and basks in the desert's beauty.

The woman tries to hide in the mass exodus of people walking back to town. As each congregation member passes her, they smile and say, "What a blessing,"

She tries to hush them, but it is too late. Looking back toward the chapel, she recognizes her husband's controlling stare singling her out of the crowd. Her lips force a smile, and her eyes divert to the ground as she slowly keeps walking.

Her husband's mannerisms ooze displeasure. Cupping his hands around his mouth, he shouts at her. "Aren't you supposed to be resting?" he asks.

"Just thought some fresh air would be nice for the baby," she replies.

"Well, I reckon that's enough, so go on and get inside now," he says.

She nervously nods, and her internal stress builds. The desert breeze lifts strands of her hair, putting a warm smile on her lips. It's the first time she has been happy since the move. Picking up her pace, her feet skip as she heads back to the uniquely patched-together village. She suddenly senses a stabbing pain throbbing through her ribs. The pain is so intense that she collapses to the ground.

Several townspeople see her crumple and rush to her side to assist. Unconcerned, the Reverend observes the turn of events from the porch and does nothing to help. Irritated by the scene, he shouts from the top of his lungs, "Carry the woman back home so she can rest. I will meet you there to pray."

Following his commands, a group of men lifts her off the ground while the women fan her with their hands. Her vision blacks out as they carry her back to the comfort of her bed. When she regains consciousness, her blurred eyesight grows clearer, and looking at her belly, she realizes her beloved bump is gone. In a frenzy, she tries to move, but her wrists and ankles have been shackled to the bed.

The Reverend rises from a chair in the corner of the small bedroom. "Well, howdy there, sweetheart. It looks like the Lord answered our prayers to awaken you."

Trying to regain her speech is difficult with her parched throat. She is enveloped in the aching sensation that stems from underneath her belly button. Her resentment builds, and her jaw clenches as she tries to free each of her limbs. "What did you do with him?" she asks.

With each brief pull of her limbs, the pain in her abdomen worsens. Glancing to her stomach, she recognizes she is still wearing the same nightgown she had fainted in, and seeping yellow-green pus oozes through the cloth, from a wound underneath.

Approaching his panicked wife, the Reverend chuckles at her struggle. "If you don't calm down now, you might rip the sutures out," he says.

She stops moving, and hate fills the pupils in her eyes. "Where is my son?" she asks.

"After that stunt you pulled, I couldn't just leave the future leader of our congregation in there," he says. Thinking back to the event, he chuckles with disbelief at what she'd forced him to do. "Letting you risk an innocent life just wouldn't have been very Godly of me."

Not understanding her husband's morbid capability, her head flinches as she locks her horror-filled eyes on him. "I will ask you again: What did you do with my son?" As she pleads, a baby cries from the adjacent room. "Alonzo! Is that you?"

The Reverend lunges forward to sit on the edge of her bed, places a hand over her pleading mouth, raises the opposite hand, and slaps her face. "Don't try my patience, woman," he says. He covers her mouth and forces her to listen as he points his finger at her eye and grins. "At this rate, you may never see him," he says.

Even though her face exudes bravery, her eyes welling tears show her true torment over losing her only child.

Removing his hand, the Reverend stands and takes a deep breath to clear his annoyance, glaring emotionlessly at her as he heads to the door. "His name is not Alonzo; it's Jericho, so beat that into your pretty little head."

The sound of the bedroom door slamming causes her to flinch. Looking to make sure he is gone, she fights to overcome the pain in her stomach as she tries to free herself.

Days pass without her seeing a single soul, other than the parishioner assigned to silently quench her thirst with one daily sponge full of water. The nights turn into days, and those days turn into weeks. As her scar slowly heals, her frame becomes frail with malnutrition. She's certain the only thing keeping her alive is the thought of one day being able to hold her beloved Alonzo in her arms. She dreams of cuddling her baby boy and having the newborn's skin against her motherly breast each night.

Everything seems right in the world until one dreadful night when her situation takes a turn for the worse, a moment she would forever hold in her bones. As her skin boils with a fever from infection, she feels her life slipping away like morning rain. Drifting in and out of a state of consciousness, her ears hear the shrieks of her child calling for her. The sound is not like the usual hungry cries she had heard through the walls before. It was different, and she knows something is wrong.

She tugs on her shackles with all her might until she frees her bony hands from the constraints. Her frail arms drag her body across the floor until she reaches a chair she can use to help her stand on her atrophied legs. Knowing she won't be able to return, she grabs a lead pencil and torn piece of paper from a desk in the corner of her room and stuffs them in her dirty nightgown pocket.

The cries grow louder, and she covers her ears in an attempt to escape their torture. She staggers down to the hall as she exits the room, searching for the child. She opens the door upon finding the nursery, and the crying stops. Making her way to the cradle, she discovers the infants' sheets are disordered and the baby is gone. As she fights back her tears, lightning strikes outside, and she rushes to the window to look at the thunderstorm.

Through the pouring rain in the distance, she can see light flickering from each window of the chapel. The image doesn't sit right in her gut, and immediately, her stomach drops. Lifting her fingertips, she touches the precipitation on the glass and whispers, "Alonzo."

Something unexplainable inside her takes hold. Some may even say God filled her soul with the strength to make things right in the world and save the child. Looking down at her abdomen, she senses her aching numbness and her fists clench with the desire for revenge.

Quickly, she opens the window and climbs outside. She hears the whinny from an old paint mare tied to the porch through the sounds of pouring rain hitting the tin roof. Looking around, she notices that during her time of captivity, the facade of every building has been restructured to look identical, and she knows she has no time to waste. Racing to the horse, she climbs on its bareback and rides toward the illuminated chapel. She picks up speed, her lengthy hair blows in the wind, and the freedom makes her smile.

As the horse approaches the structure, it slows down, quieting its steps. Swiftly, she steers it away from the windows to the backside of the building and dismounts. Tying its reins to a nearby tree, she listens as the muted screams of the baby cease. The chapel door swings open. Not wanting to be seen, she hides in the shadow of the trees and places her palm flat against the horse's nose to keep it calm.

The Reverend, flustered and mumbling obscenities to himself, exits the church and walks hastily back toward the town. Terror fills her bones as she tries to hide while he passes by. Waiting until he disappears into the distance, she sneaks around the chapel to enter through the front. As she opens the door, a flash of lightning strikes behind her and illuminates the building's interior. Rolling thunder echoes, and her knees buckle as each lightning strike reveals a more-cryptic visual of her lifeless baby boy on the altar. Crimson shades surround the table as blood drips from its wooden top and pools on the floor.

Picking herself up, she runs to her son and snatches him into her arms, swaddling him. "No, no, no!" she cries. A gash runs from the baby's sternum to the bottom of his chest, and next to the child is an old book depicting a Satanic summoning to seize a newborn's soul for power.

Staying strong, she fights back her tears as she stares at her son's filet skin. Unable to stop her emotion, a tear trickles down her cheek and falls into the deep wound. The love contained in that single teardrop causes the baby's blue-tinged hand to wiggle.

Feeling hope, she holds her child tighter to her chest. "I promise, I will get you out of here," she says. Setting the baby down, she takes off her nightgown, swaddling the child, and uses the writing supplies to craft a note. She tucks the letter away in his bindings, then runs out of the chapel door to the mare. She gives the baby's forehead a gentle kiss. "You are the only hope we have, Alonzo," she says as she covers his face with a corner of the gown.

Resting the baby on the flat of the horse's back, she feels the rain overhead stop, and she smiles. "See?" she says with a giggle to cover her sadness. While frantically securing him to the horse's back with a lead rope tied to the back of the saddle, she sees his tiny hand move underneath the covering and begins singing a lullaby. "You are my sunshine, my only sunshine; you make me happy when skies are gray. You'll never know, dear, how much I love you..." she says.

Loud yelling closes in behind her. She turns around to see her husband approaching with a rifle in hand.

His anger manifests across his furrowed brow. He fires a round into the air. "Where do you think you are going?" the Reverend asks as he continues to approach.

As her hands tremble, she plants herself and screams. "Stay away!" she says. Turning around, she whispers to her baby boy. "Just please don't take my sunshine away."

Again, the Reverend fires another round into the air.

With tears flooding her eyes, she raises her hand to the sky and slaps the horse's rump to make it run. As she watches the mare carry her boy safely away into the distance, her lips quiver.

A gunshot echoes in unison with a smile forming on her face, and she collapses to the ground.

Fourteen

The Sacrafice

1869, Whittletown

Being forced to witness his mother's death causes Alonzo to scream louder than a banshee. As he is transported back to reality, resentment escapes from deep in his heart, and his body shakes with weakness and a thirst for revenge.

Still engulfed in a haze, everything around him appears to be moving in slow motion. The outline of the Reverend contorts in front of him, looking like a shadowed bat flying through the night with his cape. "Now you know where you came from, Jericho," he says, with manic enthusiasm. The leader laughs at his weakened state. "If that no-good woman had let me finish what I started, you could have been immortal," he says, spit flying with each word. His hands lift towards the ceiling. "You could have been a God."

"My name is Alonzo and I can honestly say I have never met an evil like you. Your so close to the devil that your blood must run hotter than the fiery pits of Hell," he says.

Trying to lunge forward, Alonzo's legs give out, and he falls. As he sinks to his knees, the Reverend moves closer to whisper in his ear. "Today is the day we will finish what we started. Like father, like son, we will be powerful," he says with crazed eyes.

The words sting Alonzo's ears. "I am nothing like you," he says with a clenched jaw.

His lack of compliance angers the leader. "We can do this the easy way or the hard way, cowboy." Without waiting for a response, he snaps his fingers in the air.

The cowman drifts in and out of consciousness as the sounds of heavy footsteps approach him. Not able to distinguish the dream from reality, he senses his body levitating from the floor and his shirt and vest being stripped from his frame. He wakes upon being thrown onto the altar's surface.

As the Reverend lays the severed body parts around him, two large-statured town members shackle his limbs to the table. Fighting to sit up, the anguish of remembering his bedridden mother overcomes him.

Sounds of chaos inundate the holy sanctuary as the church members flood in to observe the ceremony. Sitting front and center is John, the peculiar man still wearing the black cowboy hat. In the first row of pews sit the men; the children sit in the middle, and the women in the back.

As the individuals take their seats, the Reverend enters from behind the door of the stained-glass confessional, and the masses clap. They point to the shackled man at the altar and chant in unison, "Sinner, sinner, sinner."

The ringleader lifts his hands to quiet them and begins his sermon.

Laying shirtless on the table, Alonzo's scar is exposed for all to see. He tries with all his energy to free himself. "Let me go! You are nothing but a mother killer!"

The leader ignores the foul words and walks in front of the altar to address the community. Raising his voice, he points to Alonzo. "Just when we thought someone had stolen him from us, he has returned. God has brought back our prodigal son."

The audience releases surprised expressions and loud gasps. "Take this as a lesson that the good Lord is capable of anything we ask, and for that, we must give thanks," the Reverend says. Bowing his head, he motions for everyone to follow.

Like a rolling wave, each one of the community members lowers their head to pray. "Let us thank God for our deliverance from all that is evil and protect us from sin. Amen," he says.

"Amen," the congregation replies. As everyone lifts their heads, they reach beneath their seats and pull out masks that match the Reverends. Raising them to the sky, they pause and continue staring forward while the women get up to assist the children in putting theirs over their heads.

While the women secure each child's mask, the leader spots John wearing the infamous cowboy hat and angrily snatches it from his head and throws it in front of the altar. His diction resembles hissing snakes, and each word's pronunciation causes him to spew saliva. "The time is near, prepare yourselves to join me in celebrating this momentous occasion," he says.

Flooding back to their designated spots, the women sit down and wait with their masks held high. In unison, all the adult men sitting in the front rows and the women in the back place their masks over their heads. Stiffening up their postures, they refrain from further movement as they unsettlingly yell out high-pitched horse noises.

Since many have never seen a horse in their lives, the interpretations are scattered. Alonzo, confused by the bizarre noises, shifts his head to see what's happening around him.

The clergyman dramatically swings his hands to tell a terrifying story as he theatrically parades down the aisle. "These are the creatures who took our redeeming son away from us!" he says. All the residents fight their terror and respond with harsh animal noises.

Spinning his body, the Reverend points back to the altar. "Who hides underneath the skin of those foul, un-cloven hoofed beasts?" he asks.

Quietly, the audience starts and crescendos their words. "Satan, Satan, Satan," they chant.

As his story builds, the Reverend glances at each of the members to verify their engagement. Consumed by the vital energy behind their chant, he continues to reel them in. His upper body bends forward to mimic distress over reliving the tale. "I witnessed their demonic behavior with my own two eyes," he says. Standing up, his hands recount the series of events. "I saw them steal my only son and shoot my dear beloved wife right in front of me."

Every word sits ill with the imprisoned man as he lies on the table, desperately tugging on the chains that bind him. Unable to free himself and having no other way to retaliate, he mocks the leader. The congregation masks his taunting with wailing noises, mourning the Reverend's loss.

The Reverend lifts his hands to silence them. "That is why we wear their flesh with pride--to remember our victory over the Devil himself. Our prayers have been heard! Just as those demons took him, they brought him back as a peace offering. Our power is infinite, and our faith makes us invincible. So, do not pity me, for that is what that sneaky devil wants. Instead, let us welcome our dear Jericho home," he says.

Alonzo's fists clench with irritation. Trying again to free himself, his right hand bumps the severed head sitting beside him and knocks it off the table. "For the last time, my name is Alonzo! Alonzo Bill!" he shouts.

As the mutilated body part bounces down the steps leading from the altar, it picks up momentum and continues to roll down the aisle. While the Reverend engages his audience with his ranting sermon, he kicks the decapitated head to the side and ignores the confined man's rebuttal. "Jericho, Jericho, Jericho!" the crowd chants.

The leader clears his throat to get everyone's attention. Once the room is silent, he reaches into his robe and pulls out a butcher knife. Slowly, he lifts the blade above his head, takes a deep breath, and, closing his eyes, begins to pray. "Let us pray. Lord, help put our times of bad luck behind us, and guided by your hand, help me rid poor Jericho of the demon the horse critter planted inside him. In Jesus's name, Amen."

Together, all the townspeople stand and raise their hands in unison to begin the offering. Taking a moment of pause, their heads tilt to look above, and their mouths open underneath the slits of their masks to stick out their tongues. Everyone holds their position and hums like a hive of bees.

The Reverend lowers the knife to the level of his eyes to admire his reflection and whispers to himself. "There can only be one leader, and he will not take that away from me," he says.

Alonzo tilts his head as far as possible to glimpse his corrupt father and winces, getting a kink in his neck. "Good Lord. You got to work on your whisper, Partner. If you were to do that where I came from, boy, oh, boy, you would get scalped. Then you would have to wear that nest on your head because of being ugly underneath," he says.

At the end of his exasperated speech, the Reverend's eyes dart to his disobedient offspring. Funneling his anger, he tightens his grip around the knife's handle. "Have you forgotten your place," he says with tenacity.

The cowboy cackles with laughter fueled by seething hatred. "Nah Reverend, I know my place and it sure as Hell ain't here. You left me to die. Thank the Lord, that I was delivered to the people that cared for me. They were more of a Father than you ever were or ever will be," he says.

Usually able to ignore it, this time, his son's condemning words trigger something inside of the leader, and he grits his teeth. "Everyone, you are dismissed! Disperse! The Devil inside of him is stronger than I thought, so I need to do this alone."

Still looking at the ceiling, the crowd's humming ceases, and they exit the building like scurrying rats. As soon as the door shuts behind them, the Reverend's pent-up frustration takes over, and he charges the altar. "How dare you make a mockery of me in front of my children?!"

Alonzo lifts his head to smirk. "Didn't know you had so many offspring," he says.

Leaning forward, the leader smacks the cowboy's grin off his face. He lets out a large breath of air to lessen the blow and lets his sarcasm take over. "Is that all you got, old man?" he asks.

The Reverend grips the knife tighter in his hand and glares at him. "For us to begin, you must denounce your sins," he says.

Alonzo turns his head to spit out a clump of blood. He smiles at the cloaked man with his blood-stained teeth. "I got none," he says.

Rage builds in the clergyman's blood.

"I know you got plenty, so why don't you go first, preacher man?" Alonzo says. His smile turns into a sneer. "You've cheated, you've killed, you've lied, you've stolen--"

Throwing his hands into the air, the Reverend hushes his son with spite. "God knows what I've done and the struggle I have had to endure to lead my people," he says. His personality shifts, and he points the knife at the tip of Alonzo's nose. "You are the heathen."

The cowboy smiles with hatred as the cold knife moves to trace his eye. "Don't be a coward. Do it. Finish what you started," he says.

The Reverend teases him with a sadistic grin by barely pushing the blade into his skin.

The feeling of the icy metal against his scar transports Alonzo back to recollections of his childhood he had buried deep inside. As his eyes spasm, he hears a distant child crying, and a mysterious force delivers him from his pain.

"Listen," a woman's voice whispers in his ear. Comforted by the familiar warmth of the whisper, he opens his soul up to the mysterious voice's message and allows his mind to remember.

"You are home," she says.

Fifteen

Blood Ties

1825, Somewhere in the Arizona Desert

The horse gallops through the night with the baby strapped to its back. As the moon grows brighter above, the infant boy silently fights for a peaceful life. Even though he is not old enough to truly understand the driving force of his heartbeat, his mother's love gives him the energy to stay alive.

The sound of a crackling fire carries for miles through the uninhabitable dusty terrain, and rejoicing, the mare releases a neighing song to announce their oncoming arrival. Setting its sights on the burning flames ahead, the horse recognizes a familiar rock formation. She lets out a whinny of excitement, ignores the aching horseshoes on her feet, and quickens her pace.

An enormous funnel of black smoke drifts from a raging bonfire, and the dancing flames showcase a collection of small huts made from earthen materials. Each has a combination of clay paste and dried straw to shelter whoever dwells inside.

As the horse reaches the remote civilization, sweat beads pool over the unkempt fur covering her lean muscles. A mountainous man steps into her path, waving his arms. The horse recognizes the familiar face and screeches to a halt directly in front of him. The charging horse's abrupt stop doesn't make him flinch as he has a deep understanding of nature and faith in the animal's communication with him.

The man steps toward the mare, his body highlighted by the bonfire's light and the full moon above. His outfit is made of light, tawny cowhides. His long-sleeved top and long pants match the moccasins on his feet. The skin showing is a shade of tan, and is weathered and tough enough to withstand the harsh sun. Each of his wrinkles shows his wisdom-filled age like the rings of an ancestral tree. Painted markings are strategically placed on his face to show his leadership position. Underneath his ornate headdress made of feathers are long braids of dark gray hair.

The indigenous man takes another step closer and lightly touches his forehead to hers to exchange thoughts. Feeling at home, the tired mare huffs air through her dried nostrils. "You are home," he says. Lifting his head, he peers around her neck. "I see you're not alone."

She whinnies and taps her feet against the hard ground. Immediately, the man senses the urgency. Using his tongue to click against the roof of his mouth, he signals that it is safe for the villagers to emerge from their huts. Men, women, and children appear and stand next to their clay shelter formations as they gawp at the visitors.

As the others stay behind, an older woman takes orchestrated steps to join the Chief. Her coarse hair flows in the night breeze and tumbles to her waist. A camel-colored dress with tiers of matching fringe that drapes to the dirt is on her body. Intricate beadwork wraps around her bodice to coordinate with the moccasins on her feet. A band upon her head is crafted from leaves, dried twigs, and colorful feathers.

They look into each other's eyes, and the man minimally nods his head in the direction of the horse's back. Without saying a word, she rushes to untie the tightly secured object. The child's toe wiggles underneath the makeshift blanket as the ropes loosen. Gently, she takes the tiny body in her hands and lowers him to the ground to unwrap him.

Her touch soaks in the baby's emotional journey, and her eyes tear as she unwraps his face. Peering directly into his eyes, she sends a message of hope. She had never been able to have a child of her own, so at this moment, she feels that her ancestors have answered her prayers.

Everyone starts to chant a welcoming call like a lightly beating drum. The woman smiles as she continues to calmy unwrap him. The voices surrounding them grow louder with a precise rhythmic timbre. As they move to the beat, the momentum causes their beadwork and fringes to dance.

As the woman peels the last cloth from the infant's belly, she howls to the full moon above, and his silent face flinches. The chanting group stops and lowers their heads to look at the ground in unison. Each starts to hum in a grave pitch to ward off unwanted spirits.

With her head tilted towards the stars, the woman joins in. Slowly, she peers down at the gash on the baby's chest and bends over the child for prayer. Her fingers gently run over the open wound, and her voice speeds up in sorrow, warding off the sadness.

The sounds of drums grow louder.

The whites of the woman's eyes become brighter and larger between her lids. As the deep drums slow their pace, she picks herself up from beside the baby boy and wraps his cold body back in his mother's nightgown.

In her final moment securing him in his warm sanctuary, she notices a piece of paper fall from a seam. Carefully, she picks up the papyrus and skims over the contents. A silent tear falls from her eye onto the page. Folding it back up, she places the note in her pocket. "Alonzo, you are one of us now," she says as she picks the child up and nuzzles him under her chin.

As his life partner carries the bundled child past the Chief, he lightly touches her back for support. Giving her a nod, he ushers her through the gathering community, and one by one, each member lightly places a hand on the boy to embrace him. The mare follows behind the parade of people and runs off to play with the village's children.

Night after night, the tribe works to heal the infant's deep wound, both physically and mentally. The tribe members hear the babies' cries from outside the Chief's hut every day. The screams are less centered around pain stemming from the wound, but are attributed to the pain from the moment he was forcefully torn from his mother's arms.

Helping the child recover from his traumatic departure, the woman set to take care of him normalizes his sorrow. Each day, she wails with him to show him her commiseration and his newfound community.

Finally, a thunderstorm rolls through the community on the anniversary of his arrival, and something shifts inside the mud hut. Everything is quiet, and for the first time, the child doesn't mourn the loss of his mother. He soundly sleeps.

The town rejoices in the child's incredible recovery and goes into the wild to forage in preparation for a feast. Later that night, every member of the tribe dresses in their most joyous outfits to officially celebrate the newest member. They patiently wait for the Chief and the family to emerge from the bungalow, and sensing the rain clear, they light a bonfire in anticipation.

At the tallest peak of the dancing flames, the Chief emerges in an all-black ceremonial two-piece outfit. Even more ornate than the outfit, his headdress is crafted from large white feathers speckled with black. Bells that jingle with each step is tied to the fringe of his soft leather moccasins. Taking his last step out of the doorway, he stomps his feet and pounds his fist against his chest. Releasing his breath, he emits a loud grunt to get everyone's attention.

Everyone gathered around the bonfire turns to face the elder and mimics his call--anyone sitting stands in anticipation.

The Chief steps to the right of the hut and turns to face the doorway. Releasing a cry into the air, he stomps both feet to direct the villagers' attention to the infant's arrival.

Just as the air falls silent, muted high-pitched jingles become louder from inside the home. Taking her time, the woman lowers her head to regard the baby cuddled in her arms as she slowly emerges from the curtained door frame. As the setting sun hits the white-and-black-speckled feathers sticking out from the back of her headband, she lifts her head to acknowledge the crowd. Single white raindrops are painted falling from the bottom of her eyelids and trailing down her high cheekbones to signify the child's rebirth.

As the Chief lifts his hands with purpose, everyone lowers to their knees to honor the child. She unwraps the baby boy's blanket, made of feathers that match her headdress, with an endearing smile. Her arms straighten to hold him in the air. "Alonzo, eager warrior," she says to the crowd.

The baby coos with glee at the bright-colored feathers and beads. His tiny chest proudly displays the reddened healing scar etched into his soft skin, and a piece of black cowhide wraps his loin as a diaper. Teardrop paintings that match hers caress his rosy cheeks and fall onto his limbs. The contrasting tones accent his unusually blue eyes. Opening his mouth, he gives a gummy grin.

The woman's hands lower to a coddling position, and her feet glide with pride.

From that moment, the people took him in as one of their own, and he became a folklore legend told to each new generation. Over each bonfire, the story would be reenacted, with two children acting as each end of the mare, returning home. A narrator would explain how the horse had been stolen by an evil pale devil who showed no mercy. When she found her way home, she brought a child with her who was meant to lead their tribe to salvation.

The woman mothering the child never disclosed the details of the letter, so it was never included in the dramatic recounts, but she always honored the words only meant for her eyes, and kept them close to her heart. He was the chosen one sent by the ancestors to complete their barren lineage. With each year of age, the boy grew more robustly svelte and learned the ropes of becoming the next warrior Chief of the village. That is where they tokened him with the surname Bill, meaning unwavering protector.

With extensive, long hours, he became the best barehanded hunter in the land. Once the skill was mastered, he became proficient in knife work and archery. It became a myth of his prophecy that the scar left behind by his near-death experience had made him indestructible, and the whispering chatter made him smirk.

Until one dry winter on his seventeenth birthday, he was given a life full of love and stability.

As the winter fell over the desert's isolation, the crops that nourished the tribe became sparse, and the village began to starve. The Chief put his people's hungry mouths before his own and handed over all reserves of harvested crops he had kept as an emergency supply. The harsh cold wasn't typical for the land, and persisted past the point of expectation.

Noticing his father becoming weak, Alonzo made animal-fur coats to stay warm as he foraged the surrounding land for food. What he was able to find wasn't enough to keep his father healthy, and before he knew it, he fell ill with a turbulent fever.

His mother developed a cough as they dealt with the Chief's death. Some said the illness wasn't brought on by the cold, but rather a broken soul tie. The only thing that kept her alive was her son's love. With each diminishing breath she took, he held her hand to give her company.

On the last day, she disclosed the letter his blood mother had left for him. "You will always be my child, but this was not the life you were meant to have. Alonzo, you are destined for greatness, and cannot die with this tribe. You must go forth and speak of us. You must avenge your birth mother and bring us glory. I had a vision where you condemned all that is

Evil. A horse as white as snow will lead your way to victory. You must believe in what's inside, and I will be with you," she says.

Sweat drips from her forehead from her raging fever. Lifting her hand, she lightly touches his chest and the thick scar. She allows her eyes to close, and her voice trails away as she passes. "Go, my son. Follow your calling and bring honor to your people and me."

For the first time since his infancy, he lets out a wail that is so powerful that it changes the weather in the sky.

The remaining villagers gather outside their huts to watch the clouds clear to reveal the sun. As the snow melts in the valley, the crops begin to revive.

Taking a moment to gather his thoughts, Alonzo finds refuge in the village's meditation hut as he prays to the ancestors for guidance. After a week of reflection, he gathers the strength to come to a decision and finds a set of ragged clothes taken from a deceased man during a past battle. Putting the foreign wear on his body, he emerges from the structure as Alonzo Bill.

Not knowing where life will take him, he says his hard goodbyes to the village that raised him and, gifting them a mare that provided him safety, he travels to a nearby mining community to discover his path. In the distance, as he gets farther away, he can hear the sound of warrior calls blessing his departure.

Sixteen

Revenge

1869, Whittletown

The powerful memories flood Alonzo's body like a trampling group of wild stallions. As he comes back to reality, his eyes roll back in his head.

Confused by the cowboy's mannerisms, the Reverend pulls the knife away to watch what is happening.

Alonzo's body starts to convulse violently, and each limb pulls on the constraints. His spine arches opposite the wound throbbing on his chest. Still under restraints, his chest slowly lifts from the table and his body starts to convulse and unnaturally quake.

The leader of the congregation's pupils enlarge, and he takes a step back. "This can't be," he says as he shakes his head.

Light projects from the tiny cut the leader inflicted upon Alonzo's torso, and his back arches even more. As the first ray of warm light hits the ceiling, the remainder of the welted zigzag left of his stark-white scar boils. The pent-up light waiting behind the sealed skin furiously strains to be let free. The pain of the healed wound being pried apart causes the cowboy to scream.

Bewildered at the scene unfolding, the cult leader becomes spooked and takes another step back.

The scar tissue tears open little by little, and the light of Alonzo's soul shines out to protect him. While in excruciating pain, his shaking head lifts to look around, and he sees three figures standing next to his feet at the end of the sacrificial table. His blood mother stands in the nightgown she had taken off to save her child, along with his adoptive mother and father in the black cowhide outfits they had worn to the baby's revealing ceremony. Their presence brings static to the air and strength to his bones. As he tries to look in their eyes, he notices their pupils are gone, and the pain from his tearing wound forces his head back to the table.

In synchrony, his guardian angels each place one hand on his trembling legs, and a flood of light causes the scar to rip the rest of the way open.

Fighting back the pain, Alonzo's brow drips sweat and his mouth springs open. As his esophagus readies to release a howl, another funnel of bright light exits his throat. Immediately, the blood running through his veins simmers, causing the shackles to melt off his extremities.

Dumbfounded by the series of events, the church leader uses the handle of the butcher knife to scratch his head through the itchy mask.

The cowboy's mouth abruptly closes, and his eyes turn back to the Reverend, full of hatred for the evil that has been done. His nostrils flare as he sniffs the air, and the smell of burning metal makes him smirk. Abruptly, though still lying stationary, his head turns to face the man who tried to kill him.

At once, the presence of the newfound energy causes the cloaked man's bones to shake.

Sitting up, Alonzo looks down at his gaping, bloodless, wound and sees his beating heart. Quickly, he closes his eyes to meditate, and as he opens them, the cut has healed.

The shocked Reverend takes another step back with confusion. "Impossible," he says.

Refocusing his energy, Alonzo's eyes fixate on the man who was eager to take his life. "You murdered my mother and left me for dead and you call yourself a man of God," he says as he swings his legs off the table. The Reverend's eyes grow wide as he watches the decomposing body parts cascade to the floor.

Alonzo shifts his weight on top of his feet, and straightens his back, one vertebra at a time. Looking down upon the touted leader, his breath becomes heavier with disdain. "God has spoken and you shall pay," he says as his right hand lifts to the sky and his fingers snap to call for his cowboy hat. With his palm open, the felt brim of the black hat lands in the middle of his waiting hand, and he returns it to the top of his head.

As he looks at the masked man, he extends his hand and signals with his fingers for him to come forward. The reverend's ghost-stricken eyes scan the room in a panic for ways to escape. As he sees the only exit is behind the cowboy, he runs for it.

Enjoying the comedy, Alonzo watches the evil man fearfully sprint past him and chuckles deeply. "Where do you think you're going, Reverend?" he asks. His fists clench with the horrific memories and energy from the surrounding spirits that have suffered at the clergyman's hands. "I believe you still have some sins to confess and account for.

The man continues to scramble for his escape. "I said stop!" Alonzo shouts as he lifts a hand out in front of him. As his hand's palm flattens, a large crucifix shakes on a wall near the altar.

Reaching the door, the Reverend gives a few tugs and realizes it has been locked. Slowly turning around, he lifts his hands and pretends to surrender. Unable to hide his disdain, he spits on the ground in front of him. "Go to Hell," he says.

The cowboy smiles. "Maybe if you are lucky, I'll meet you there," he says.

As his left hand shoots forward to join his right, the crucifix flies off the wall behind him and impales the Reverend clean through his sternum. The wood's impact drops the evil man to his knees.

Alonzo watches the man retch as his mouth generously spews blood. The heels of his boots loudly clunk and each spinning spur clinks against the wooden floor as he approaches to take a closer look. "That's for what you did to my mother," he says.

Picking up his pace, he hovers over the Reverend. His foot lifts from the ground and pushes the cross deeper into his chest. "Reverend, my ass! A man of God wouldn't do the things you've done. I reckon your nothin but a murdering, mangy cult leader," he says as his boot kicks the man over.

Slowly bleeding out, the Reverend looks at the church's vaulted ceiling, and his breathing takes on a gurgling sound.

Placing his boot over the man's throat, Alonzo pushes down on his windpipe. "My name is Alonzo Bill, and I am here to punish you for your sins." As he applies more pressure, the Reverend gasps for air.

Without warning, the church's front door forcefully bursts open, and every remaining member of the evil community floods inside. The crash immediately causes Alonzo's gaze to shift as he bends down and pulls the blood-soaked crucifix from the dying man's chest. "I reckon y'all are here to pay your respects."

As they see their beloved leader dying on the ground, the group of crazed men and women, screaming like a pack of wild hyenas, charges at the cowboy. Jumping over their leader's body, they move closer, screaming at the top of their lungs. "Get him!"

The trained warrior arises from Alonzo's soul, and his lips take on a confident grin. Seeing everything coming at him in slow motion, he seizes the cross, throwing it like a Bowie knife and impaling the first approaching man. He grabs him as he falls forward, extracts the cross, and uses the man's body as a shield as he continues to stab the others who follow closely behind.

After annihilating the first line of crazed individuals, Alonzo retreats to the altar, cross in hand, and, biding his time, begins chucking body parts at the approaching angered followers. Several remaining congregation members begin retching. Alonzo grabs the severed limb holding the paintbrush and rips the stitched wooden handle away from the skin. He shrugs at the sight of a stray finger still attached and breaks the wood against the altar, creating a sharpened stake and charging the intruders with the paintbrush in one hand and the crucifix in the other. "Time to meet your maker!" he shouts.

Two monstrosities of men race toward him first; as they swing at him, he stabs each simultaneously. As they fall to the floor, a group of women runs toward him with fierce hatred.

Holding the bloody weapons, Alonzo stops in his tracks and motions for them to stop. "Whoa, hens. I was taught better than to evoke violence on a female," he says. His hands remained raised.

They refrain from listening and release high-pitched angry shrieks. The first woman lunges forward and, using her nails, deeply scratches his side. "This is for the Reverend!" she says.

As Alonzo winces, he hears his mother's whisper in his ear. "They're not women anymore; the devil's got them," she says.

The women watch him turn his head to address a figure they can't see. "I can't, momma. They still look like sage hens," he says.

"Find the courage, son," she replies.

As the cowboy turns his head to ask them to stop once more, the pack descends, clawing, kicking, and slapping him. Battered and bloody, rage fills his eyes, even harsher than before. Powered by all his force and that of his ancestors, his arms swing forcefully in a spontaneous state of fury with the sharp objects in hand.

Catching his breath, he wipes the droplets of blood from his eyes and scans the church for survivors. Across the way, one beastly-looking man remains. Quickly, Alonzo recognizes the fellow from the pack of bystanders when he was carried to the church, it is John. Despite still feeling a bit irritated from when he had stolen the cowboy hat off his head, he notices something peculiar about him when compared to the others.

He is not immersed in the surrounding events, instead, he stands over the dying Reverend without mercy. Having the time of his life, he hysterically laughs as he kicks the man with his dusty boots. "Who's stupid now?" he says. Kicking harder, he steps on the Reverend's femur bone and slowly releases his body weight. As the bone snaps, the man lets out a scream, and he laughs.

The cowboy looks at him and slowly claps his hands in applause. The man stops what he is doing to look at the approaching cowboy.

"You know, you're not as yellow-bellied as I thought," Alonzo says.

Turning his attention to the reverend, the man cocks his foot back and gives him another kick. "Take that! On account of you killed my pappy. You're a bad, bad man."

"He killed my momma, so I understand," Alonzo says. Slowly getting closer, he gets an idea. "Say, partner, on account of he killed both our parents. What do you say we shake on a deal?"

The idea of someone including him perks up the man's ears, and he stops what he is doing to listen. "There anyone left in town?" the cowman asks.

Quickly answering, the man shakes his head no. "I reckon the rest ran when they heard the yelps. You, me, and the Reverend are the only ones left, far as I know," he says as he peers at the bodies strewn across the floor.

Pleased by the news, Alonzo slowly takes off his cowboy hat. "What would you say if I left you in charge for a moment, like the Sheriff of this here church?" he asks as he places the cowboy hat on his head.

John's eyes light up with excitement. "Oh, golly gee. I've never been in charge before," he says.

Interjecting, Alonzo points to the Reverend. "All you got to do is make sure that fool doesn't leave those doors right there," he says as he motions to the exit.

John feels empowered and adjusts his posture. "You got it, boss," he says. He gazes back down at the man by his feet, and a grin returns to his face.

Racing out the door, Alonzo turns to face him. "Enjoy yourself. I owe you one, partner," he says.

Happy he can give John an opportunity to serve justice on the man responsible for his tragic loss, Alonzo runs to the town, smiling at each scream echoing behind him. "That-a-boy," he says with a snicker.

When he reaches the storefronts, the abandoned dirt road resembles a ghost town. Having no shirt and torn blood-spattered pants, Alonzo makes haste to peruse the shop windows to find one displaying a western get-up that interests him.

All the display windows are designated for different items, and each store has nothing the same. As he walks by the leather shop he had been dragged from, he spots the corpse he'd added to the display and analyzes the rest of the leather wear surrounding him. "Hate to admit it, but you've got the best selection. Sure is a shame that you had an unsavory personality and a wobbling jaw."

Setting his ego aside, Alonzo quickly enters the shop and grabs a new pair of black suede chaps and a matching vest. He gets carried away as he admires the rest of the shop's accessories. Not giving a care, he strips the rest of his clothes off to change his pants and boots, then finds a shirt to coordinate with his all-black color scheme.

A fly lands on the corpse's open eye in the window, and the sound of its wings buzzing catches the cowboy's attention. The outside light reflects off the silver roping around the man's hat's brim.

"All right, don't have to pull my leg to get my attention," he chuckles. Doing a two-step over to the case, he plucks the hat from the dead man's head and places it on his own. "I reckon I earned it."

The road is eerily quiet. The only form of life is a tumbleweed trying to escape with the help of a gust of wind.

Alonzo tips his hat to shield his eyes from the dust-filled glare as he leaves the shop. Trekking back to the chapel, he notices a house smaller than the rest positioned at the end of the row nearest the church. The structure makes him feel uneasy, and without a second thought, his feet lead in its direction.

Slowly, he approaches a dusty window and peers inside. Within the confines of the walls, he spots a baby cradle with light-blue sheeting covered in cobwebs. He sees a window that leads to the adjacent room. Still carrying the crucifix, he tucks it under his belt loop and uses his hand to clear the dirt from the glass pane to get a better view. To his horror, he spots a bed with restraints still attached.

It's his childhood home.

His blood begins to boil. Seeing the bed where his birth mother had been held hostage causes a stream of hatred to fill his head and his eyes to sting with anger. He moves to a third window and notices an oil lamp, on a table in the corner of the room. Using the rocker on the front porch, he smashes the glass and climbs inside.

His hands tightly grab the handle of the lantern and a couple of matches from the table as his anger causes his eyes to blur. Climbing back through the window, he strikes a match on the window casing, lights the wick, and tosses the lamp through the broken glass, setting the house on fire. The flames move like a wildfire through parched timber. As it burns, he steps back to observe the bittersweet moment, and with the release of a single tear, he quietly sings, "You make me happy when skies are gray. You'll never know, dear, how much I love you."

Feeling his mother's presence makes him smile.

A large gust of wind feeds the flames, blowing them in the direction of the town. "Please don't take my sunshine away," he says as he watches the town turn into an inferno. The sight of the city burning and ash falling from the sky like snow in winter puts a grin of contentment on his face. Satisfied, he brushes off his hands and heads back to the chapel.

The setting sun gives the desert a peaceful glow, and the flames make each strand of his golden hair glisten. As his tired legs pass through the chapel's picket fence, he spots a shovel's blade reflecting light as it lies parallel to the ground by the freshly tilled garden. He grabs the handle and drags it behind him.

As he nears the church steps, he hears two troubling gunshots. Confident he will open the door and see that his partner-in-crime has finalized the reverend's fate, he enters with a toothy smile to commend him, but his eyes are met with disbelief.

Instead of finding the predicted scene, he discovers John sprawled out on the floor with a look of death in his eyes. Upon further examination, he finds two bullet wounds in his chest. At first, he cringes, but then a flashback occurs of the reverend's ruthless killing of the four men who had carried him to justice, and he has an epiphany: the preacher wasn't wearing his holster, leaving him with only the six-round chamber in his revolver. With John's killing, he would be clean out of bullets.

Knowing there is no threat of a firearm, Alonzo takes his time to pay his respects to the dead man lying at his feet. "I sure was warming up to you." Lowering himself to the floor, he brushes his fingers against his eyelids to close them. "Rest in peace, John," he says as he scans the room for the hiding Reverend.

He sees a boot sticking out from under a pew midway up the path to the altar. He reaches down to retrieve the cowboy hat and takes a knee, gently placing it on John's chest. Standing, he notices a trail of blood smeared along the hardwood floor. Like a traveling slug, the Reverend left behind a blatant trail of bloody slime, making it easy to find him.

Alonzo pretends to be hunting, acting as though he doesn't know where he is. "Reverend, where are you?" he asks as he looks down every row of pews, skipping the one where he is hiding. He grins at the dying clergyman's heavy breathing and takes a moment of pause to build the anticipation.

Without warning, the cowboy hops in front of the sheltering pew closest to the door and surprises him. "I reckon you're as crooked as a dog's hind legs," he says.

With his last burst of energy, the masked Reverend lifts the revolver with his shaky hand, pointing it at Alonzo.

Leisurely, the cowman swings the shovel above his head as he approaches.

As the Reverend pulls the trigger, the empty chamber of the gun sounds a *click, click, click, click, click, click*. The clergyman, realizing he has run out of options, panics as he tries to crawl away, dragging his broken leg.

The cowboy quickens his pace and reaches down to grab hold of his mask. "I want to see the light leave your eyes," he says with a sneer as he pulls the matted horsehair from the Reverend's head and throws it to the corner of the room. His face twists with disgust. "You are even uglier than I imagined," he says.

Clutching the shovel with both hands, he feels his jaw tighten. "Got any last words?"

As the Reverend tries to build sympathy, he pretends to stutter. "I-I reckon I sure am sor--" he says.

Before he can finish his falsified apology, the cowboy lets out a scream of rage and thrusts the shovel's blade into his neck.

With each inch that the shovel lodges deeper into his flesh, streams of blood shoot in every direction from his severed arteries, miraculously missing Alonzo's new outfit. With one final heave, the Reverend's head pops off and rolls a bit before stopping face-down next to the cowboy. "Hope Hell treats ya well, pop," he says with a snicker.

Wiping the sweat dripping from his brow, he assesses the carnage scattered through the church. "This is bout' to be more work than uncorkin' a Bronc."

The sound of a stray rooster's crowing outside signals the stroke of midnight and the turn of a new year.

"Hallelujah, another year without the California collar," Alonzo says.

Seventeen

Above Snakes

1870, Whittletown

Alonzo sinks deeper into the cushioned velvet seat in the confessional.

And just like that, we are back to the beginning.

He chugs the remainder of the moonshine left in the black bottle and drops the empty container to the floor as he tries to clear his mind. He belches and, with blurry vision, begins analyzing the inside of the box where the Reverend spent the bulk of his day. Taking his time, he allows his slow-focusing eyes to scan each inch of the wall. "Got anything else to tell me?" he asks.

Parting the silk curtains adorning the walls, he discovers drawings on papyrus lining the darkened room. The sketches reflect an influential male leader taking over a Podunk town with a small, helpless population. Illustration by illustration, the scenes progress with a final image of the clergy leader donning wings and floating above the masses, his head adorned with a Godly crown.

Intrigued, the cowboy leans forward to take a closer look, tracing each lead mark with his finger.

In front of the levitating preacher is a blood-stained sacrificial altar. A depiction of a shirtless man that vaguely resembles Alonzo lays dead across the table with blood dripping from his mouth and a scar running the length of his chest, gaping open, his chest cavity emptied. The preacher hovers over him with his heart in his hand, devouring the vital organ.

The scene sends jitters from Alonzo's head to his boots. He releases his hand from the curtain, allowing it to conceal the disturbing view. "Sure has quite the imagination," he says.

Overwhelmed by his emotions, he chalks up his sadness to thirst and redirects his attention to finding more booze.

He scans the corners of the small room and a stack of papers catches his eye. "I'll be damned. Now why on God's green earth would the Reverend have a heap of my wanted posters?" he says, as he reaches down to pick up a copy. Suddenly, a light flips on in his head as he realizes that no self-respecting lawman would give a reward of a second helping of communion.

Lowering himself to his knees, he scrambles on the floor and, using the palms of his hands, feels in the shadows for hidden compartments. "Come out, come out, wherever you are."

Outside of the elaborate box, the chapel's windows darken with the day's progression, and the clouds turn an odd shade of blueish gray.

The light fading makes it harder to see even with the window broken and door ajar. He pats his sides for his coin pouch, sticking out his tongue to aid in his concentration. As his fingers fumble inside the bag, they contact a familiar rough-edged box. "I knew you were hiding in there all along," he says as he pulls out his lost box of matches. He takes out the makings for a cigarette and places the roll-up in his mouth. Chuckling, he pulls a match from the box, and using one of the drawings on the wall for friction, he strikes it against the paper. The burning tip adds a bit of light to the room, and he realizes he has torn the last picture in the sacrifice-progression lineup and shrugs. "That one wasn't very realistic anyhow," he says.

Using the tiny flicker of light, he searches underneath the upholstered seat and sees the outline of a small box concealed next to the wall.

His eyes light up with the excitement at the possibility of finding treasure barely out of his hand's grasp. He lies on the ground, wiggling his tall, lean body under the chair to get closer. Still holding the fading match with his left hand, he grabs the box with his right and begins scooting out from under the chair. His stomach crawling against the floor causes air bubbles to form in his stomach. Without thinking of his surroundings, he rears his head up to belch and hits the back of his skull on the underbelly of the sturdy chair. "Dang, my melt!" he says as he winces and his hat tumbles to the floor. As the chair settles above him, each leg vibrates to find its balance.

Alonzo shimmies from under the velvet throne, dragging the box with him. The combination of alcohol, crawling, and rubbing the goose egg on his head causes him to forget the match in his hand, and it tumbles to the floor. He puts the hat back on his head to cover the welt and moves his focus to the box.

The sudden smell of smoldering wood causes his nostrils to flare. Smoke builds quickly underneath the seat cushion and, within moments, fills the tiny room.

He begins to cough uncontrollably as his lungs fill with fiery fumes.

"Jiminy," he says as he attempts to cover his mouth with his palm. His eyes burn from the pollution in the air, and he squints to find the exit.

He carefully grabs the box and crawls on his hands and knees to escape. Upon exiting the suffocating room, he frantically tries to catch his breath. Flipping his body to sit on his hind end, he scoots further away with the wooden box on his lap.

The smoke thickens inside the confessional and funnels through any cracks to escape. It becomes so thick that it produces a foggy haze that consumes the surrounding floor. Deep orange light fills the inside of the sin box as the flames grow taller.

As fire voraciously engulfs the holy artifact, Alonzo's eyes widen in disbelief. Knowing he only has minutes left before the fire takes down the chapel, he scrambles to his feet and runs for the door, feeling an immense sensation of heat building behind him.

Without looking back, he jumps headfirst through the doorway and chucks the box out in front of him. Loud explosions from burning ammunition sound behind him, propelling his body faster toward the unforgiving ground, and he somersaults to lessen the blow of his fall.

Ash disperses into the air and falls like rain onto the graveyard. Large chunks of burning cinders are carried through the air by wind gusts to land on the freshly dug dirt. One by one, the whittled grave markers go up in flames.

Curled in a ball, Alonzo uses his suede-covered arms to protect his head from the falling debris, then peeks through his protective limbs to survey the damage. Seeing that the explosions have subsided and the catastrophe has been reduced to mere flames, he uncovers his head. Scanning the ground around him, he encounters a severed hand with a missing finger next to his boot. His body jumps, and he clutches his heart. "Jesus, friend, you must have slipped my mind," he says.

The flames persist, turning the chapel into ash, as he stands and uses the spur of his boot to make a hole. Nudging the limb with the toe of his boot, he taps it into the shallow divot and kicks dirt to cover it. "Good as new. Hopefully, you get to paint in heaven with all your limbs," he says. A grin softly forms on his sediment-crusted face.

Turning to look at the chapel, he gives a slight wave with his hand. "A*dios*. Don't let the door hit you where the good Lord split you. Your mangy filth is cleansed," he says as he performs the sign of the cross through the air.

The flickering flames reflect off the wax-polished light-colored wooden box, calling for his attention, pulling him like a fish to a baited hook. Giving in to the beauty glistening in his eye's corner, he turns his body to look. His intoxication seeps through his skin as his fingertips caress the carved edges, and a hiccup exits his throat.

The polished cherry-wood exterior sides depict a harrowing story of warfare, complete with impaled bodies and violent scenes of bloodshed. As he focuses on the mysterious chest, Alonzo discovers the lid's latch was broken open upon the fiery landing. As he lifts the cover, exposing the contents, a genuine smile of happiness consumes his face. "The only thing better than booze," he says.

Inside the treasure chest rest two forged revolvers with silver carvings of horses and wood accents on the grips. Black pieces of silk wrap around each of the barrels, keeping them in pristine condition.

Basking in the glory of finding treasure, he takes his time to relish the moment. Resting on the backs of his heels, he carefully unpackages the weaponry. Holding the guns in the air, he turns them from side to side in an attempt to capture enough light to analyze the carvings.

The sky opens above his head without warning, and an off-kilter orange ray of light shines between two gray clouds and onto his fingers. Feeling the warmth against his skin, he closes his eyes and takes a deep breath. As he releases his lungful of air, his gaze rises to the heavens, and he tips his hat in a show of appreciation. The sky above roars with the sound of crackling thunder.

A drop of rain touches his cheek, and he lowers his eyes to survey his hips as he tries to figure out if the new artillery will fit in his holsters. He glances back to the wooden box and, digging under the silken pieces, finds black-leather belted holsters and a hoard of bullets. He smiles from ear to ear. "That will do the trick," he says.

Making haste, he pulls the belts from the box and fastens them around his hips. Next, he kisses each revolver, loads them with bullets, and secures them in the confinements of the holsters. Filled with satisfaction, he smiles while tucking the rest of the ammo into his coin pouch.

The sunset falls behind the clouds of the bone-dry terrain, and the light of the bright sleepy sun turns a purple hue as the remaining smoke drifts across its fading brilliance.

Knowing the town was behind the wanted poster, he takes a moment to reflect and gives thanks. As he admires the beauty of the surrounding land, he rests his hands on his new six shooters, daydreaming about fresh beginnings. He closes his eyes tightly and prays to the sky above. "Just give me a sign, and I will do whatever is asked of me."

As the last word of his prayer finishes, a horse whinny is heard in the distance, creating a sound that echoes across the desert.

Alonzo forces his eyes to remain closed to wait for a sign, taking the sound of the horse as a delusion and his mind playing tricks on him. As he tries to ignore the illusion, he hears heavy hooves swiftly approaching. Concern about unwanted company coming to join him causes his eyes to spring open. His hands dart to prepare for a shootout and rest with building anticipation on the tops of the guns resting on his hips.

The whinnies become louder, now accompanied by prancing feet. Spinning around to meet the intruder, he draws his weaponry and comes face to face with a rearing white stallion. He drops his hands to his sides and rushes to the creature. Unable to contain his excitement, he embraces its neck. The steed nuzzles his nose into his shoulder and neighs with jubilation at seeing his long-lost friend.

Trying to remain manly, Alonzo pushes himself away from the horse and scrunches his face to fight back his oncoming tears. His hand lifts to his sniffling nose, and he clears his throat. "I reckon I told you I didn't want to see your ugly face ever again," he says. Unable to keep a straight face, he smirks before rolling with laughter. He slaps his knee as his chest bounces from the deep-bellied chuckles.

The stallion picks up his hooves to mimic his companion and lets out another whinny. "I'm just tussling with you, old pal. You know I didn't mean what I said. It was only me trying to protect you," Alonzo says with a shrug. Tears stream down his face from laughing too hard. He uses his hand to wipe them dry as he stares at his faithful companion. "Boy, am I sure glad to see you."

Licking his soot-covered face, the horse's gaze shifts to the remnants of the leftover buildings. "Yeah, it looks worse than it is. Lucky for us, we got a long ride home. It will give me plenty of time to fill you in on what you missed," Alonzo says with excitement.

The creature lowers its neck for the cowboy to hop on. Grabbing onto its lush mane, Alonzo mounts on top of the horse bareback and pats its neck. "All right, partner, lead the way," he says. Bonded as one, the pair of friends trot off into the night.

Some say that to this day, if you listen closely, you can still hear the cowboy telling his outlandish tales about his long ride home.

Eighteen

My Dear Alonzo

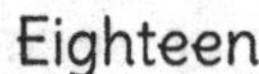

To the finder of my sweet baby boy,

I pray to God that this letter finds you. If it has, you have found my very flesh and blood I sent off into the night. Alonzo is the little boy swaddled here with eyes bluer than clear water. Please don't bother to find his home. I reckon it may seem sad, but he has none to come back to. By the time you read this note, I'm sure they will bury me. My life was put at risk to save this bundle of joy.

Let me be clear that neither of us has had an easy life. I grew up without a mother to look up to and a father who ran a small church. Reflecting upon it, maybe that was why I married a Reverend myself. I was born in a town where the church was the community, and sacrifice was required to pursue happiness. Like every young girl making the exchange into womanhood, I wanted to marry, and the best option for me was the child's father.

He seemed decent in the beginning. That was, until we moved to the small town he called Whittletown.

We found a chunk of barren land and built it up. Boy, was that taxing on our poor fingers. I remember nights of doing the brunt of the work with little help. While I was chopping wood, my husband would be practicing his future sermons to recite to his congregation.

Traveling by word of mouth, we got a community built off hope for something different in a world full of sin. At first, I thought the new members were good people and they would help offload some labor. Then, I realized they only fueled the evil inside my husband's heart. The more members we got, the more I saw his personality change before my eyes. He was meaner than a hungry rattlesnake trapped in the winter snow. To teach a lesson to the churchgoers, he would punish me to set an example.

Sometimes, that meant locking me up in the shed like a mangy critter. Other times, it meant a lashing or two. I noticed no punishment was ever the same for the same action he had told me the devil helped orchestrate. Still, I thought I deserved it, and I put up with the treatment he gave me. No one in the town said a word about his actions.

I never understood how our population continued to grow. The town had little to offer its residents. We would constantly have droughts and food shortages because the land was too dry to farm successfully.

I planned to run away and leave my horrible life behind until I was blessed with my sweet baby boy. Realizing I could not leave him fatherless, I had to leave my childish feelings behind and stay.

As my belly grew, my husband's anger followed. Each day, I would be told what God felt I should do with my daily actions and how not to ruin his early life. This included walking, eating a lot of food, and expressing my opinion. Anytime I would choose to go against his wishes, I would pay the price. I thought later in my pregnancy, it would get better, and he would show more mercy, but I was wrong. It showed me the disregard he had for both me and the offspring I loved so deeply.

The worst day came towards the end of carrying my son. It was scorching-hot inside our home confines, so I went to walk in the breeze, and he caught us. My stomach dropped when I heard him call my name. At that moment, I didn't know if he would end my child's life or mine. The worst part was watching the church members leave the service past me and not even bat an eye of concern. Every one of them sheep was privy to what was happening, yet no one helped.

I was alone.

I woke up shackled to my bed with the precious bump stolen from my belly. He had taken everything from me. As I lay helpless and in pain, he visited my bedside to condemn me for putting our son in danger. He blamed me for my predicament, but it was clear that his despising nature was the only reason for my torture and my stolen child. He was a jealous, controlling man who didn't want a son. A son grows up to be a man, and the Reverend did not take a liking to the thought of another man rivaling him as the omnipotent. The man enjoyed telling others what to do, but ran from others' criticism.

I was in grave danger as soon as that child exited my womb, and being my most precious flesh and blood, I had no choice but to do everything I could to save him. Tied up with no food or water, I would listen to his helpless cries in the other room and try to escape. Months of the torture passed before my body no longer wanted to fight. Mentally, I did. It was just that my body was weak and wanted to sleep.

Stuck in the same set of clothes I had been chained up in, I lay awake, waiting for death to greet me. Shutting my eyes, my ears were flooded with the cries of my baby boy. I reckoned something wasn't right, and this time, my husband would kill him. Unhinging my bony wrists from the bindings around my wrists and ankles, I grabbed this piece of torn paper with a pencil to write a note, if I could only send him away to freedom.

Not finding my boy in his room, I headed out the window for the chapel. To come to my baby's rescue, I took the gentle mare my husband gave me as a gift for working hard. After hiding in an overgrown tree, I waited for my husband to leave and went in to see what had happened.

What I witnessed, I would not wish on any mother. As the thunder grew outside, I saw my boy, whom I had held close to my heart, dying on the altar table. My husband had fileted him like a cut of meat and left him to bleed out. Next to the child was a book filled with hateful spells, the plagues of Satan.

At that moment, it was apparent time was running short to save my sweet child's life. I wanted him to taste the freedom I never could.

I was convinced there was hope for him, and when his fingers wiggled, there was not a doubt in my mind that he was meant for something bigger than the town that held him captive.

Having nothing to help stop the bleeding, I wrapped him in the nightgown off my back and quickly wrote this note to hide inside. I swear I could have never written faster if my life depended on it.

After sending my child to you, I know I will suffer at the hands of death, and I am agreeable with that. I won't die in vain, but for a child I believe in. Please, take care of my sweet baby boy. He has done no wrong. He is a victim who has suffered because of my choice. I beg you to take him in as your own and make my last breath worthwhile.

Just don't try to find the town he came from, or me. By the time you read this, I will be safely watching from above.

-I am indebted to your kindness,

His Mother

GITTE TAMAR

Brigitte, "Gitte," Tamar was born in a small rural
Oregon town. Growing up, she was enthralled by

scary tales featuring poetic tones and consistently gravitated towards writing darkened narratives.

In Ten-Cent Man, Brigitte explores the stigma behind societal stereotypes, and how, when straying away from others' expectations, an individual can indeed find themselves. Formatted in an old western setting, she has lived for writing this psychological thriller with dark comedic twists. She believes that the key to enjoying every moment is to be true to yourself.

www.ingramcontent.com/pod-product-compliance
Lightning Source LLC
Chambersburg PA
CBHW010845190726
48286CB00012BA/2995